A NO EXCEPTIONS NOVEL

the
Lover's
Secret

J.C. REED

Copyright © 2014 J.C. Reed

All rights reserved.

All rights reserved. No part of this publication may be reproduced, distributed or transmitted in any form or by any means including photocopying, recording, or other electronic or mechanical methods without the prior written permission of the publisher.

This is a work of fiction. Names, characters, places, brands, media, and incidents are either the product of the author's imagination or are used fictitiously. Any similarities to persons, living or dead, is coincidental and not intended by the author.

Trademarks: This book identifies product names and services known to be trademarks, registered trademarks, or service marks of their respective holders. The author acknowledges the trademarked status and trademark owners of all products referenced in this work of fiction. The publication and use of these trademarks is not authorized, associated with, or sponsored by the trademark owners.

Cover art by Larissa Klein

Editing by Shannon Wolfman, Autumn Conley & Edee Fallon

ISBN: 1500670464
ISBN-13: 978-1500670467

To all who love and are loved:

In life there are rules; in love no exceptions. The heart is a castle of glass. Sometimes we're tempted to invite someone in, not to see them stumbling upon our deepest secrets, but to see if they care enough not to break it.

- J.C. Reed

NEW YORK CITY – Present Day

ONLY TEN MINUTES to go.

Big, white snowflakes fell from the darkening November sky, coating my hair as I walked past the empty benches in Central Park. Even though dusk hadn't yet fallen, the street lights were on, casting their soft, golden glow on the white-speckled path.

My high heels made hardly a sound as I trekked through the thin layer of snow covering the asphalt. With each step I took, my heart raced faster in my chest. The blonde wig hid my chestnut locks and stood in strong contrast to my little black dress, making me feel like someone else. I wrapped my coat tighter around me, even though the fabric was too thin to stave off the cold wind. It really didn't matter; my on-edge nerves had me boiling inside.

This was it…the big night I had been waiting for.

I couldn't wait to play the game. I couldn't possibly get there fast enough.

Eager to get to my destination, I urged myself forward, hurrying my pace toward the busy streets of New York City. Only a few more minutes, and I finally reached the hotel. Men turned their heads as I strode into the luxury foyer and shrugged out of my damp coat. The snug little number I had borrowed from Sylvie, my best friend, was so tight it kept riding up my thighs, garnering even more stares. The material was as thin and light as silk, and so low cut that anyone who cared to look would catch an ample glimpse of my cleavage, but at least it wasn't transparent. The dress, coupled with sinful, seven-inch heels and stockings that hugged my legs like a sheath, made me feel like a hooker and completely out of place; almost as if I didn't belong in this expensive hotel that screamed old money and high society—a rich world that was foreign to me.

I stood out like the proverbial sore thumb, and not just because of my clothes—or the lack thereof. Simply put, my outfit wasn't something I wore every day, or ever. But I'd really had no option. Today was an exception, because the instructions had been clear:

Wear something provocative.

So I had selected something daring from Sylvie's skimpy wardrobe. Not the most daring ensemble, but the one that would still fulfill the request without making me want to hide behind the nearest tree.

With a sigh, I draped my coat over my arm, and then held it up to my chest in a weak attempt to hide some of my exposed cleavage as I made my way across the foyer to the back.

The doors to the club were wide open. I breezed through them, barely acknowledging the curious glances of the bouncers, and stopped for a moment to familiarize myself with the interior rooms. The club was dimly lit and carefully designed with elegant, upholstered chairs facing a long, narrow bar area. To my right were what looked like private tables, as well as a circular dance floor with mirrors hanging from the ceiling. Everything sparkled and shined, polished to perfection. The entire atmosphere screamed money and sex. Even the air smelled forbidden. All that seemed missing was a troupe of half-naked dancers I assumed would arrive soon enough.

And then my glance caught *him*, and my breath remained trapped in my throat.

He was sitting at the bar; his beautiful face, framed by his dark hair, was turned away from me. His gaze was glued to the glass in his hand and the swirling, golden liquid inside it. Dressed in a tailored black suit that did nothing to hide the perfection of his sculpted body, he was sexy, no doubt about it. But what really drew me to him was the mystery surrounding him. Even from across the room, I could tell instantly that he was the kind of man I would never have gone for a while ago. The kind of man I would have invited into my bed on a whim. He was the kind of man I wanted to fall under my spell.

I strolled over and perched myself on the bar stool near him. Far enough to watch him without giving the impression that I was desperate for company. Close enough for him to notice me. I crossed my legs, purposely allowing my borrowed dress to ride up just a little bit higher. The barman took my order, and for a moment, I turned away from the hot stranger. The next thing I knew he was gone.

Confused, I swept my eyes around the half-filled room, but there was no sign of him among the other patrons. Disappointment washed over me at the prospect that my outfit might not have been sexy enough to attract him to the extent I had expected.

Game over before it had even began.

With a dissatisfied sigh, I turned my attention back to my glass.

"Are you looking for me?" a deep voice with the slightest hint of a Southern accent whispered behind me, caressing my senses like an exhilarating summer breeze.

I sat up straight but fought the urge to put some distance between us. His voice was so sexy, a delicious tug formed inside me. Something much deeper pulsated within my core, urging me to play my cards right this time. I turned around ever so slowly, my gaze searching his, and for a moment, I was rendered speechless at the naughty glint in his eyes.

Wow.

Talk about stunning.

Barely a few inches away from me stood the man I had watched earlier. As he stepped nearer and his hands brushed mine, my skin began to tingle. He was so close I could feel his hot breath on my lips and the heat emanating from his delicious body and light bronze skin. His shoulders were broad and his arms looked like they could carry a woman where she belonged—in his bed—but the most stunning feature about him were his dark green eyes that reminded me of haunted woods covered in morning dew, and lush meadows.

Eyes so beautiful, they had to be made of sin.

Was it the varied shades of green that gave the impression? Or his irises that looked like cracked stones on a beach? People always said the color green was calming, but it wasn't calming at all. It was like a wild garden inviting you to run in only to trap you and never let you go.

I had never met someone with eyes like that—the kind of eyes that made me want to do crazy things such as dress like a stripper and give him a lap dance. There was a hunger in them—a strong power to devour my soul and my heart. Just prying myself away from them was hard, as if the hypnotic pull was too strong to resist. Or maybe I didn't want to. If looks could have undressed, I would have been stripped bare, naked and spread on top of a blanket, wearing nothing but a smile on my lips, and pleading with him to make me his.

"I'd love to have a drink with you, Miss, uh…" His eyes caught the credit card in my hand, and he held it up to read my name slowly, as if he were examining a rare bottle of wine he was about to savor. "Brooke. Miss Brooke Stewart."

My heart skipped a beat at the way he spoke my name. I tilted my head to one side, narrowing my eyes.

"And you are?" I asked in mock disinterest and the most serious tone I could muster.

Gorgeous, boyish dimples formed in his manly cheeks as he smiled and sat down on the bar stool next to me. He was uninvited, and yet he couldn't have been more welcome. As if sensing my unraveling, his lips slowly parted, revealing two strings of white, perfect teeth I would have loved to feel on my skin.

He held out his hand. "No need to know it," he said.

"After tomorrow morning, I'll only be a memory for you anyway."

Wow. Talk about blunt.

I smiled sweetly and inclined my head to regard him. "In which case, forget I ever mentioned mine."

"I doubt I'll be able to," he whispered. "After tomorrow, you might just be the only thing I'll be able to think about, Brooke."

My name rolled off his tongue in a sexy, rumbling way. Ever so slowly, his fingers clasped around mine, and his head dipped low again, so close I could feel his breath on my ear.

"I couldn't help but notice your sexy legs, Miss Stewart. Surely those high heels must be painful. How about I show you my room, so you can take them off? We'll order drinks, get to know each other, and do something about that pain of yours."

He was right; I was in pain, but it wasn't coming from my shoes. My whole body ached with a yearning for him to touch me, begging to know whether the sexual tension between us would actually translate into mind-blowing sex. I loved Jett's little games and their culminating finale.

As though sensing my thoughts, he pulled back, but he didn't let go of my hand. His eyes kept probing mine with an intensity that made me swallow hard, and blood rushed in my ears as I watched his lips curve into a lazy, lopsided smile that instantly melted my panties, metaphorically speaking. Just looking at him, I felt drugged, as if the chemical reactions in my brain were some complex cocktail of sex-fueled hormones, waiting to diffuse.

He had that effect on me, yes, but I harbored no intention of letting him know it. If he wanted me, he would have to do more than shoot me that arrogant, self-assured smile my way. In all honesty, there was no way I'd get involved with a man like him—not when I already had accomplished half my goal. He had seen me, and I had let my guard down a bit. Now, I had to figure out how to get away.

"As flattered as I am," I said, smiling politely, "I'm afraid I'm not interested. Now, if you'll excuse me, I have other business to tend to." Evading his heated gaze, I grabbed my bag and turned away when his hand clasped around my upper arm—gently but forceful enough to stop me. His touch was hot, burning through my clothes like lava.

"Why not?" he asked, wearing a lazy grin that spelled trouble.

The way he was standing, so close to me, with his hand around my arm, I felt myself heating up. His thumb started to move in circles over my skin, carrying with it an unspoken promise I couldn't deny. A picture flashed through my mind: his lips and tongue licking my skin, his fingers prodding my knickers to find my secret entrance. Instantly, the telltale heat of a major blush scorched my cheeks.

"Are you scared because I'm secretly turning you on?" he asked. His hands moved lower, down my spine, until he reached the small of my back. It was just a small, almost innocent move, but his confidence overpowered me. "Or is it the prospect of me entering you that arouses you?"

I stopped his hand from wandering further south and laughed nervously as I tried to push the pictures of his exploring fingers inside me to the back of my mind.

"In your dreams, perhaps," I said, sounding much more weak than I intended. My attempt to brush him off was a feeble one. And, judging from his wide grin, he knew it.

"I don't believe you," he said.

"Of course you don't," I muttered, and neither did I.

Get a grip, Stewart. Act like you're not interested. Play hard-to-get.

"I don't usually get involved with strangers," I stated as emphatically as I could, my voice betraying me with its trembling.

A devilish glint appeared in his eyes.

"I wasn't suggesting a date," he said with the same confident tone. "It was a proposition—sex and nothing else. What I'm offering is something you've never experienced before. You seem like a practical woman, but you're also curious. I can tell by the way your eyes keep glinting, challenging me to keep this up until your resolve crumbles. You want me to push you hard enough to the point you can't bear it anymore."

I swallowed hard, because he was right. "What if I'm married, with five kids and a husband waiting for me?"

"I highly doubt that." His eyes scanned my face, my half-exposed chest, and then slid lower, until I could feel the heat of his gaze on my legs. It barely lasted a second, but the brief span was enough to send another delicious pull through my abdomen. Eventually, our eyes connected again.

"I don't see a ring on your finger, Miss Stewart."

"Maybe I left it at home," I suggested weakly.

He inched closer, pressing his hands down on the bar beside me, until his lips were mere inches from mine. He was so tall I had to lean back to look all the way up. But it wasn't his height that intimidated me; it was that confidence of his, bordering on an inflated ego. I knew what kind of man he was. Men like him loved hard and played just as hard. I wanted to love hard for a night, but could I take the heat?

"If you left it there, you did it on purpose." He made it sound like a fact. His lips twitched, and I couldn't help but stare at their luscious perfection: lips I wanted to kiss and nibble on; lips I wanted to kiss me back; lips that would make me scream his name.

"What are you saying?"

"You're here for a reason."

I raised my brows, feigning surprise. "And what reason would that be?"

His lips moved closer, and for a moment, I thought he might kiss me. An electric tingle washed over me as he whispered in my ear, "Excitement, action, sex—all three, which you so obviously, desperately need today." He leaned back and tucked a stray lock behind my ear, then continued slowly, "You're looking for someone to give you a new sense of reality, someone who will help you forget your crappy day at work and take you on the ride of your life." With each word, his deep tone sent another ripple of hot lava through me.

"You make it sound like I'm a cheater."

He shook his head and leaned forward again. "No, not a cheater. More like someone who's bored with her life and works too hard."

His hot breath tickled my neck, and my thighs clenched in lust. I wanted him to kiss me, but more than that, I wanted him to take me.

"I can offer you that and more, Miss Stewart. All you have to do is join me in my room, which is conveniently located upstairs."

I forced a scowl. I knew I should try harder to brush

him off, but there was something about him that entranced me, and it was more than just the promise of getting what I had come for. I was captivated by his voice, his touch, and the hard masculinity of his body.

Fight, Stewart. You're giving in too soon, too easily.

I moistened my suddenly parched lips and smiled. "I know what kind of man you are."

He lifted his eyebrows in mock interest, but said nothing.

"What makes you think I'd choose you when there's a whole club full of potential suitors?" I asked. "Maybe I'm looking for a neat guy, a nice guy, who doesn't usually break the rules, someone conventional and not hell bent on winning another set of panties."

He chuckled, his eyes still on me. "Because you can sense my secret," he whispered. "I *never* disappoint. One night with me will give you the kind of excitement that lasts a lifetime. While I cannot promise that you'll climax just once and not want more, I can promise you an unforgettable night, Miss Stewart—an incomparable night, I might add, and your only regret will be every second we wasted without sex."

Oh boy!

His confidence was so huge it ought to be listed as the world's biggest in Guinness Records. But was it working? Hell, yeah. It was working far better than I wanted to admit.

My heart pounded in my chest as I watched him pull out a keycard from his pocket and place it in my hand.

"Room 521," he said with a smirk. "Be there in twenty."

"I'm not coming." I shook my head, just in case he hadn't heard my weak voice.

He smiled, revealing sexy dimples that urged me to touch them. "Of course you will...and I promise I won't bind you to my bedpost, at least not for the entire night."

The mere suggestion aroused me, and judging from the way his lips were twitching at the corners, I was sure he knew that and was feeling the same way.

"Twenty minutes." With that, he picked up his coat and left.

Craning my neck, I followed his broad shoulders. Only after he disappeared in the crowd did I turn around. A laugh escaped my lips.

"Dammit," I muttered under my breath and stood from my bar stool.

He wasn't just eye candy. He was pure sex, a conjurer of wicked naughtiness. He was a paradise for lady sinners, and I was about to be one of them. I knew it just as well as he did.

Of course I'd join him. After all, a bet was a bet, but first I'd let him simmer a bit, let him think I had ditched him. Maybe my resistance would put a little dent in that big ego of his. I was certain he was completely self-assured I'd play along and join him in his room. Maybe he had kept his voice low on purpose, so I'd chase after him, go in search of him, or whatever would give his ego another boost. Maybe he thought there were no exceptions to his rules, but things would be different today. Today, I was going to be the only exception to his game, because I had no intention of losing to the likes of him.

Chapter 2

THREE MONTHS EARLIER

I SAW IT long coming—the moment my nightmares became real and my fear would unleash the worst in me. As much as I tried to forget all the things that had happened, I couldn't. A part of me kept thinking back, hesitating, doubting that the past was over, always wondering if there was something that I could do. Doubt and hope were like a disease—invisible, but always present. Ever so small, they would grow to immense proportions, bringing with them nothing but chaos that would draw me in. So deep that I knew I could lose myself, and make me hate myself for all the things I could have done but didn't.

Falling into the trap was one of them, as was defending myself and hurting a guy in order to escape.

Maybe if I had allowed him to rape me instead of trying to hurt him, maybe I wouldn't be in the mess I was in. Instead, I found myself trapped in the staircase, my heart racing so fast, I was sure I'd die from fear.

Liz had been right.

I should have followed their orders and commands. I should never have tried to get away. Now I was fighting for my life and I had to get away, or I'd be killed.

I yanked at the emergency exit door. It was locked. A curse escaped my lips.

Shit.

I couldn't retread my steps, back to *them. To him and his friends.* They would never forgive what I had done. They couldn't get me. Not now. Not when they were so angry with me. I had to act quickly. There was no other option but to try and find a way to escape. Get out of the place as fast as I could.

Forcing my legs forward, I started to climb up the stairs. My breathing came hard and ragged. My blood rushing unnaturally loud, I took two steps at a time as fast as I could until I stumbled and grasped the railing for support. I cringed at the sound. But it was too late.

The door leading from the corridor into the stairwell opened with a loud bang.

"Bitch, I know you're in there," he yelled. "Keep running all you want, but I'll get you eventually, you little slut. And when I do, you'll pay. You'll wish you were never born."

His pounding steps echoed through the air as he picked up his pace, his laughter ringing in my ears. Soon he'd reach me...if I didn't find a door. Any door I could open and lock behind me.

My body trembled so hard I was sure my knees would buckle under me. But my mind remained surprisingly sharp as my eyes swept the place. To my right was a door leading into the third-floor corridor. I opened the door and darted through, making sure to close it behind me, then stopped again to scan the area. There were more doors, most of them closed. I opened the first door to the left and entered what looked like a storage room with lockers.

Footsteps thudded up the stairs. He was getting closer. There was no doubt about it. Soon, he'd be checking the corridor, opening and closing doors in his quest to find me, like a hunter going for the kill.

There was no time for running. I had to hide.

Without thinking, I yanked open the door to a locker. It was big enough for me to squeeze in. This one had to do. I pushed myself inside the confined space and pressed my nails into the thin slits to close the locker door, holding my breath as I strained to listen.

My whole body shivered. My breathing just wouldn't slow down and seemed to echo as loudly as a train. If I didn't calm down, he'd hear me. I pressed a hand against my chest and took measured, shallow breaths, silently praying for a miracle that I'd survive.

The thudding of footsteps rose in volume. He was coming closer. And then the door burst open and the thuds carried over, filling the room. I squeezed my eyes shut and held my breath to stifle the whimper forming at the back of my throat.

He was in the same room as me. I could hear him loud and clear through the drumming of my heart. Rivulets of sweat began to trickle down my back until my skin was slick with moisture. I had never been more afraid in my life, not even when I had woken up to find myself kidnapped and trapped in a cell with no way out.

Eventually, I dared open my eyes and through the tiny slits, I glimpsed him. His bulky size was blocking the doorway and his face, now bathed in shadow and light, looked both threatening and menacing.

I began to count in my head.

Seconds passed and seemed to stretch into minutes. Finally, he departed and the door closed behind him.

He was gone.

I breathed a sigh of relief.

He hadn't found me.

I was safe. No, not safe, but at least I was alive and still had a chance to escape. I began to count again. As I reached one hundred, I started from the beginning, and once more. Everything remained silent. Now was the time. Better now than later...when his friends would return to help him search for me. In my state, I couldn't possibly outrun or fight off a few of them.

With shaking hands, I opened the locker and stepped out in the hope that one of the doors in the corridor would lead to freedom.

Freedom.

I liked the word because it was just like a promise: free of pain, fear, and danger.

I had almost reached the end of the corridor when hands grabbed me with such a force they squeezed the air out of my lungs.

He hadn't left. Just like the hunter he was, he had waited for his prey to come out of its hiding place. I struggled against the iron grip when he kicked me so hard my head hit the wall and everything turned black.

"Where do you think you're going?" he hissed and his fingers entangled in my hair, pushing me down onto the floor.

My scalp began to burn as waves of pain began to shoot through my body. But I wasn't ready to give up yet. I had every intention to fight as long as I lived. So I kicked as hard as I could, but he was faster and stronger.

He growled and muttered something. My attempt to kick him was rewarded with a punch to my face. I shielded myself from the impact. Before I knew it his hard fingers curled around my throat and cut off my air supply.

He bent forward, shaking his head. "Little bunny. Look what you force me to do. Let's hope you'll be worth the trouble." His cold eyes showed no mercy as his fingers pressed hard on my windpipe.

My vision blurred. From the periphery of my eyes, I saw a second guy kneeling next to me, and holding a syringe in his hand.

A friend of his had arrived. They were going to drug and rape me, like they had done with Liz. Then they would kill me for having defied their orders. I just knew it.

"No, please no," I wanted to beg, but no sound came out.

The needle pierced the skin as easily as a scissor cutting through paper.

It was too late.

All my fault. I should never have tried to escape.

I should never have challenged a killer.

I should never have attracted his attention.

The drug began to course through my veins. My body grew weak almost instantly while my heart continued to slam against my ribs. Slowly, darkness descended upon me.

The sound of tearing clothes echoed through the air.

I was losing everything. The battle. The control. Myself.

And then a gunshot pierced the air and someone said, "I'm sorry, Brooke. We'll get you out of here." A deep voice I faintly remembered from somewhere. But where? I fought to put a face and name to the voice when he shouted, "Call for an ambulance, Brian."

I'm safe, I thought before I fell into darkness.

If only it were true.

Chapter 3

NEW YORK CITY – Present Day

ONE OF THE most interesting things in life was the certainty that nothing would ever remain dull for too long; sooner or later, the unpredictable happened. The trick was standing aside long enough, watching how a set of things and people came together in random patterns that weren't really so random at all, and witnessing how that collision resulted in a burst of new experiences for everyone involved. Good or bad, those experiences brought failure or winning a new meaning.

Just like the green-eyed guy who would be my date for the night.

At least that was what I thought when I headed for the bathroom to reapply my makeup and regain some of my composure. With one last glance in the mirror, I took a deep breath and walked out.

Now that I had his attention, it was time to move to Plan B.

The lobby had filled with evening guests. Turning a corner, I almost bumped into a man who was standing near a big palm tree planted in a massive fiberglass flowerpot.

"Sorry," I muttered and turned away when he looked up from his newspaper and, as our eyes met, a sudden shudder ran down my spine.

He was dressed in a striped business suit. His dark brown hair was parted perfectly, combed neatly to one side. While his somewhat old-fashioned hairstyle and affordable looking clothes weren't the reason for my ignited attention, I couldn't stop the sudden alarm ringing inside my head because of the way he regarded me. Most people barely paid me a fleeting look; some guys checked me out. But this man's glance was different. It was a little too sharp, too hard. It was almost as if...

No, don't go there, Stewart.

I stifled my paranoia. Too many bad things had happened. It was time to let go because it was over. So what if a man had looked at me in a weird way? That didn't mean he was a bad guy. No one would ever come after me again.

Now, if I could only just believe it...

As if sensing my unease, he returned his attention to his newspaper and continued to read whatever he'd been reading before. An instant later, a woman joined him, and relief washed over me. *Probably his wife,* I figured from the way she kissed him on the cheek, and together they walked to the reception desk, their arms linked, their chatter indistinguishable.

Stupid paranoia.

It had happened before, and it just kept happening. For the umpteenth time, I pondered whether or not I should pay my therapist another visit. The trouble was, I hadn't seen him for eight years, and I still felt guilty over the way I had so abruptly broken off our sessions when I decided I was strong enough to deal with the issues of my past myself. He had insisted I wasn't ready, but I had brushed off his concerns, claiming he didn't know me as well as he thought he did. Yet, on a subconscious level, I knew even then that he was right. But I wanted to feel normal, and if I visited a shrink again, it would be like admitting to myself that I was corrupted. Branded. Damaged beyond repair.

Since I couldn't bring myself to visit him again, the best thing I could do for the time being was remember his advice: *"Try to focus on the things that feel real, things you can grasp."* The hotel seemed like a good start. Taking three deep breaths, I forced my mind to let go of my mistrust of the people around me and instead focused on my surroundings.

Passing through another hall, I marveled at the exquisiteness and luxury of the place. The TRIO wasn't just one of the most expensive hotels in New York City. Rising over Manhattan's premier shopping and business districts, it was a popular see-and-be-seen place for the rich and famous. From the huge indoor water fountains and the magnificent crystal chandeliers hanging from backlit onyx ceilings to the stunning displays of each hall I passed, I realized calling it an image of perfection was no overstatement.

The place *was* pure Zen. It made me wonder how life was for the VIPs of the world, for those who weren't too shy to spend thousands of dollars a night in such luxury accommodations, just to wake up each morning to the knock of someone bringing a three-course breakfast or to spend half their day at the spa that occupied an entire floor.

It wasn't the life I had been born into, nor was it the life I needed to be happy. But I could certainly see the appeal and why it might be alluring, even for a day.

Or even a night with him.

Excitement washed over me as I stepped off the elevator, onto the fifty-first floor and stopped in front of Room 312. Soft music carried over from inside—perhaps a TV set or radio. I swiped the keycard, unsure if I did it the right way, but it didn't work. I took a deep breath and knocked softly.

Nothing stirred.

I knocked again, this time a little louder.

Finally, the music was switched off, and the door was thrown open.

A guy stepped out.

I frowned. Just like my prospective date for the night, this man was in his early thirties and dressed in an expensive business suit. The only problem was: I had no idea who he was.

"You're early," he said, opening the door wider to let me in.

My gaze traveled past him to scan his room. I took in the open notebook on the table and the loose sheets of paper spread haphazardly around a glass of what looked like scotch or whiskey.

"I'm not paying extra just because you're early," he mumbled, and a whiff of alcohol hit my nostrils.

What the heck?

I took a step back as realization kicked in. "Sorry. Wrong door. I, uh…" My words failed me. It wasn't at all how I had imagined my first one-night stand would go down. How could I explain to this man that I wasn't at his service, in a situation so mortifying I could barely talk? I thought it over for a second, then decided being short and prompt was the way to go. "Sorry again...and have a nice evening," I muttered and turned my back to him when he blocked my path.

"Wrong door? That's about the lamest excuse I've ever heard. You know that?" He sounded affected, maybe even annoyed, but a mask of friendliness remained on his face. "You chat me up online, only to leave me hanging. Why would anyone pay in advance for a stripper?" He paused for effect.

I just shook my head, signaling that I had no idea.

"Correct me, but I thought we had something. You wanted to meet with me here, so here I am."

I groaned inwardly; he was taking my rejection personally. I couldn't avoid the low chuckle escaping my lips.

Me, a stripper?

The very idea of me being a stripper was hilarious. In a way, it was a compliment; while I had the curves, I lacked the long legs. Besides, I could barely swing a few dance moves.

"I understand your confusion, but it's clearly a mistake," I explained.

His eyes lingered on me, pondering, and I caught another whiff of alcohol. "Is this some kind of game you're playing, part of the act or something?" he finally said, taking another step forward. "You know what? Forget what I said earlier. I'll pay for the extra time. Now just move your hot ass inside and give me what you promised the other night." His hand went around my waist, close enough to touch my ass, as he pointed behind him.

He has to be kidding.

For a moment, surprise kept me glued to the spot, until I realized that my amusement could easily be mistaken for flirting, particularly in his alcohol-induced hazy state of mind. But it was too late to tell him that. His hands grabbed my ass in what seemed to be some sort of bizarre encouragement to join him. I pushed him away a little harder than intended. Hurt crossed his face, and for a moment, I actually felt sorry for him. He hadn't been rude, and he was clearly confused.

"Listen, I'm not who you think I am." I held up my guest card. "See? I'm not playing games. I really did just knock on the wrong door. Now, if you'll excuse me and keep your hands off me—"

"What's going on?" a deep voice resounded behind me, cutting me off.

I turned to peer at my actual date heading for us—in a hurry. A breath of relief escaped me...until I caught his expression.

Oh shit!

He was furious.

And by furious I meant he was close to turning into a

raging bull.

There was no need to ask him how much he had seen; the throbbing vein in his temple said it all. His face was an angry mask as he headed straight for the poor man. I stepped in front of my date, but before I even got the chance to explain, he shoved the man back against the wall with no questions, no explanations—just like that.

I stared, still glued to my spot, rendered speechless.

"What the fuck, dude?" The man stepped toward him, raising his hands in the process.

For a moment, I was afraid they might start throwing punches; I was entirely opposed to any form of violence whatsoever, but there would be little I could do to stop it if it ensued. If I didn't know any better, I would go as far as saying that stopping a fight between two testosterone driven men would be as hard as breaking up a fight between two pit bulls.

"Don't you fucking touch her again." My date poked his finger into the guy's chest, as if the venom in his voice had not carried enough threat.

Standing next to my date, the man looked small. He looked up into my date's angry face, and then his glance moved back to me, as if it was all my fault. "She's my goddamn stripper," the guy said. As laughable as it almost was, in the midst of the palpable tension, he was still adamant that I had to be there for him. "I paid for her, man. It's her job to please me."

"Are you fucking joking?" my date barked. He roughly grabbed the man by the collar and shoved him back against the wall. "Does my pregnant girlfriend look like a stripper to you?"

The guy's hesitant gaze brushed me from head to toe, lingering on my tummy.

My date's forearm muscles tensed a moment before he yanked at the man's collar hard—so hard he forced his gaze away from me.

I wanted to point out that being three months pregnant was nothing. I was hardly showing. If anything, I looked slightly bloated, as though I was struggling with constipation. Instead, I said, "It's clearly a misunderstanding, Jett. Let it go." I tried to pull my date away, but he didn't budge. Rather, his grip on the man's collar tightened so hard I was sure the fabric would tear any moment. I sighed. Ever since we had found out about the pregnancy, Jett had been more overprotective than ever.

"You apologize to her before I decide to smash in your face," he growled.

"It's not necessary," I whispered, but they both seemed to ignore me.

A moment passed, during which the man's alcohol-induced haze seemed to lift a little, and his eyes cleared. Finally, he held up his hand. "I'm sorry. I didn't realize," he said, then apologized some more.

I didn't hear the rest of what he said, because my date grabbed my hand and forced me down the hall, toward the elevators. I shot a glance over my shoulder at the man as he walked back inside his hotel room and slammed the door shut.

After the elevator carried us one floor up, I followed him down the hall to his room. The silence was unnerving. I looked at the door number and realized my mistake: I had confused the numbers 321 with 312.

Jett pulled out his keycard and swiped it. The door was hardly closed when he turned to me in the narrow hall, his eyes ablaze with fury.

"What the hell were you doing there, Brooke?" he asked. His height was both menacing and arousing, his hard body taking up all available space.

What was that? Did I detect a hint of jealousy?

I regarded his face, the way he was working his jaw, his posture rigid and tense, and then I shrugged. "I just…got lost."

"You could have called me. The fucker was about to drag you into his room and do God knows what."

I knew it was true, and there was no need to comment. Still, we were supposed to play a game, pretend we were two strangers meeting each other, so Jett could later pretend I had my first one-night stand with him, and now the game was ruined.

"Nothing happened." I shrugged again, signaling that it didn't matter. "Just let it go."

He rubbed a hand over his face in frustration, but after a few moments of silence, his shoulders finally relaxed.

I looked at the man I had come to know well over the last few months. Jett had never been one to show much emotion, but now that I was carrying his child, everything had changed. "Will you always react like this?" I asked, frowning, so I wouldn't laugh out. I had to ask, because Jett had never struck me as someone with anger management issues; then again, I knew firsthand that people seldom wore their psychological problems on their sleeves.

"Only when I spy a damsel in distress, and especially when said damsel is mine." His lips twitched for a second, and he inched closer, wrapping his arm around my shoulders. "I'm sorry for erupting like that. Are you okay?"

I shrugged again. "Of course I'm okay. I was doing fine. There was no need to threaten and scare the guy over a simple misunderstanding," I said. "The poor man will probably be scarred for life now, and I'm sure he won't be booking services on the net anytime soon."

His features hardened; clearly, he didn't appreciate my weak attempt to infuse some humor into the tense situation. "Serves him right for believing you're a stripper."

"Can you blame him?" I pointed to my dress that was

shorter and thinner than anything I had ever worn before. "Look at this getup."

"Look, baby, even if you tried, you still wouldn't look like a stripper. You're sexy as hell, but you don't look cheap. Any guy who would even suggest otherwise deserves an ass-kicking." He shrugged out of his jacket.

I said nothing, but couldn't help but stare at his broad shoulders, admiring the way his muscles seemed to strain his shirt.

"The guy's an asshole with no respect for women. Someone should have taught him a lesson a long time ago."

"Hmm." I dropped my handbag on the counter, then walked over to him. My hands traced his strong chin and the tiny spot he had missed while shaving.

He smiled, as if the dark fury had simply vanished at my touch.

I loved the way I was able to influence my boyfriend's mood like that, and my heart skipped a beat at the thought. I still couldn't believe I could call this sexy man my boyfriend, and I couldn't believe I had such an effect on him. Pleased, I leaned back against the wall and posed seductively. "But that's not why we're here, right?"

He got the hint straight away. "You're damn right about that." Ever so slowly, he inched closer, with a devilish glint playing in his eyes and a wicked smile on his lips, intimidating but stirring the deepest pleasure. "You think you have what it takes, Miss Stewart?" he asked, instantly getting back into character. He pinned me against the wall with his arms and moved his mouth dangerously close to mine. With an appreciative growl, he leaned into me and whispered, tracing my ear with his hot breath, "You've come to the right place now, and that's all that matters."

Absolutely.

I smiled. As always, Jett Mayfield was sexy without even trying.

His mouth descended hungrily upon mine, and I shivered with unbridled pleasure as our tongues merged in a first, heated kiss. I trembled even more when his skillful fingers slowly made their way under my dress, dancing across my flesh, ready to still the aching pain within my core.

Chapter 4

"WAIT! AREN'T WE going a little too fast?" I asked, prying my lips from Jett's. My heart slammed hard against my rib cage, and my voice sounded hoarse. We were spread out on the floor in the middle of the hall, with him on top of me, our legs intermingled. His broad chest obscured the view of the remaining room, but I wanted to see it. A one-night stand would be great, and I knew I could pull it off, but I needed a little warm-up—maybe some chatting or getting to know each other.

Not too much, just enough to make me feel less...cheap?

I groaned inwardly as soon as the thought wafted into my mind. It was the voice of reason, and of course it was saying exactly what I did not want to hear. Jett was my boyfriend and all, but my first attempt at a one-night stand, even a pretend one, had to be done right.

"I thought you wanted this," he said matter-of-factly.

I nodded. "Yeah, but...well, I thought you'd give me the tour first."

"The tour?"

"I'd like to look around the amusement park a little before I hop on the rides," I said with a wink.

Our eyes connected, and a flicker of playfulness appeared in his gaze. "A tour of this room is the least I'll give you." A slow smile spread across his perfect lips.

I raised my brows impatiently.

He sighed, then stood and reached down to help me up. "Fine. Then let me show you around first...and then I'll take you."

Holy cow.

He knew how to woo a woman. No need to beat around the bush.

I squealed as he slapped my backside playfully, and followed him. As we breezed through the door, I stopped to stare. Ever so slowly, my mouth dropped open.

Calling it a hotel room would have been a major understatement. Jett's accommodations looked much more like a presidential suite, with at least four luxurious bedrooms and adjoining bathrooms. The living room was decorated in gold and cashew hues. It was furnished with a marble fireplace, a huge plasma TV, three large couches, and various cabinets and side tables. A black piano adorned the far east corner, right next to the floor-to-ceiling windows that offered a majestic, panoramic view of the city, which would invite any overnight guest to stare for hours.

I would have gawked a little longer if it weren't for my date insisting we move on to the library and a spa room. Opposite the spa room was the master bathroom. Everything—from the walls to the ceiling to the sinks and even the huge bathtub—was made of polished marble that glistened and sparkled under the bright lights.

"Wow." I let my gaze brush the expensive furniture and décor before settling on Jett's majestic body. He fit right in, like a king in his castle.

"And there's the master bedroom." He pointed to the closed door at the end of the hall, and I assumed he'd saved it for last with a good reason. He cocked an eyebrow and flashed me a grin, in case I missed the insinuation dripping from his voice. "I'd say this is the main attraction."

No shit.

My smile matched his grin. "You might just be spot on about that." I looked at the closed door and wondered just what kind of amusement I'd find on the other side.

This was it—the reason I came here.

With my heart pounding hard, like a marching band in my chest, I opened the door and walked into the dimly lit room. Just like the living room, it offered stunning views of the skyline. I tried hard not to look too impressed by the ivory silk-covered bed and lush furniture or the hundreds of twinkling ceiling lights above the bed. It was hard not to imagine our bodies tangled in silk, panting and moaning while the soft fabric caressed our senses. It was even more difficult to control my breathing when those fantastic, flashy pictures of us naked entered my mind. I could see myself lying on the covers, touching him, his mouth on mine, my legs wrapping around his narrow waist, pulling him deeper inside me as my hips moved in accord with his. Or maybe we could do it on the floor, where the thick, fluffy carpet would tickle our backs as our hands roamed free, and I could gaze up at those starry lights and—

"Like it?" he whispered in my ear.

For a moment, I couldn't tell whether he was talking about the room or the movie playing in my dirty mind. His deep voice nearly made me jump, and almost caused me to take a step back to put some distance between us.

"Try…love it," I said breathlessly.

"Good. I've booked it for two nights. I know you said one night only, no strings attached, but I figured you can't possibly get enough of me in one night."

Ah, the magnitude of his ego. How the heck could he possibly squeeze it through the door?

I turned to face him, my skin prickling.

Two days? No way.

"This place is too expensive, Jett. Besides, I thought you were going for an average hotel room, not the Taj Mahal. Why would you book a place like this? A normal room would have been just as fine. We didn't need a suite."

"Why not? What's wrong with it if I can?" Jett laughed. "This is a special occasion, Brooke. We deserve a special room for a special woman like you."

His hand began to trace the contour of my arm, then settled on the small of my back. His touch was light, making my skin tingle, yet it defined the moment as if he thought he had a claim on me. And maybe he did. Just not yet.

I was going to play hard-to-get.

"It's just money," he continued.

Just money? Sure. If you've got it, why not spend it, right?

I had to laugh at how easily it came to him.

"What?" He shrugged. "I want us to have a good time." The hairs on my skin rose as he leaned forward until I could feel his warm breath against my neck. "Besides, it's not a suite," he whispered, pointing toward a door I hadn't noticed before. "It's a penthouse—the largest they have. And I intend to make love to you in each and every room...twice."

It was my turn to shake my head. "Now there's a lofty goal," I said.

Men and their impossible ambitions.

Maybe the guy had enough money to keep him afloat forever, but my bank account was in desperate need of a cash infusion. For weeks, Jett and I had been working together to expand and rebuild his company, all on a tight budget and under new management. I would have been game if it weren't for my new job and the fact that I, as the project manager at Mayfield Realities, was on a schedule and crazy busy. After we put a huge scandal behind us, the company was slowly but surely gaining a reputation for excellence, and new clients were flooding in by the day.

Unlike Jett, I hadn't been born into wealth. I had been taught from an early age about the value and importance of working hard and living frugal. He didn't know what it meant to be poor, though, so there was no point in sharing my ideas about how to save money, one of which was not to throw cash out of the huge windows by booking the most expensive suite, the largest penthouse, in a hotel. Still, I knew he meant well, and I was ready to let him give us a good time.

"Ready to see the rest?" His face was still unfazed, but there was the slightest hint of impatience in his voice, the kind of voice that told me to get moving so we could get on to the more important things.

We walked into another, larger living room, where there was a second black piano and a huge terrace that overlooked the twinkling city lights. The room was different. Its red wallpaper screamed sex, power, and sin. A modern, round sofa faced a fire in the middle of the generous open space, like a small gladiator arena. The rug looked soft, and there was plenty of room to make love on the floor, right between the fire and the sofa.

Hungry flames leapt at the thick log, illuminating the entire room and mirroring the inferno that was burning inside me. In the silence, I watched how Jett's sexy body moved across the room, confident and enigmatic, as he made his way to a side table and retrieved a bottle of champagne from an ice bucket. He poured a glass for each of us and handed one to me before we snuggled on the sofa. He raised his glass for a toast. "To a special night together."

My lips curled into a smile as I lightly clinked my glass against his. "Thanks." I took a sip and let the tasty, bubbly liquid roll over my tongue. It was sweet without being overly sweet, and it reminded me of grape juice, with just a hint of jasmine.

"Nonalcoholic," he explained. "It's a bit different."

I nodded, even though I wouldn't have detected the difference, but I appreciated that he was considerate of my pregnancy. I smiled at the way he took another sip, his perfect lips pursing slightly to assess whether he could get used to the sweet taste or not. He hated the taste of jasmine, and I bit my lip so I wouldn't laugh out loud.

"This is crap," he murmured, grimacing again. He turned back to me and said nothing more.

I took another sip and eyed the fire. "I like it."

"That's because you're sweet. A good girl." He grinned at me.

I cocked an eyebrow. "And you aren't good?"

He inclined his head. "Not so much. I'm probably the bad boy your mom would advise you to stay away from."

How true.

In fact, that had been exactly my first thought when I first met Jett Mayfield.

"I'm not really nice," I whispered. "I can be very blunt."

"That's fine," Jett said. "I have a thick skin, which is perfect for handling fire."

His green eyes regarded me with a hunger that made my cheeks flush with heat. He was too tall, too strong, too masculine. Next to him, I felt tiny, helpless, a state I had never felt before I met him. His sleeves were rolled up to his elbows, and his tie was gone. My brain told me to keep things casual, but my fingers itched to touch his hard body, and my tongue wanted to lick his skin.

Not yet. Too soon. Talk. Get to know him, as if he's really a stranger.

That had been the plan all along. If I gave in to his advances first, I'd never get him to open up and let me be in control.

"Is that some kind of famous painting?" I pointed to the framed artwork hanging on the west wall, a painting of blue and golden swirls.

"I doubt it, but if it is, I'm sure it's just a replica. I much prefer originals. They're always worth having," he said, his gaze lingering on me for too long. "I like the real thing."

Holy pearls.

He was flirting with me, making it hard to engage in small talk. How the heck was I supposed to keep my cool when all I wanted was to fuck him on the spot? Biting my lip, I forced myself to calm down. I didn't need alcohol to feel the effects he had on me; his presence was enough. Combined with his aftershave, the way he was regarding me, and the sound of the crackling fire, it was a deadly and sinfully sexy combination. In every way, he was the epitome of beauty and perfection, mysterious yet alluring—and most of all, he was mine.

Chapter 5

"WHAT NOW?" I asked as the silence became uncomfortable, spiked with anticipation.

"You'll see."

He was so relaxed compared to me, and I knew he was doing that on purpose. Except for a sparkle in his eyes, I detected no nervousness whatsoever, but then Jett had mastered the skill of keeping up a straight face when he wanted to keep his thoughts hidden. As well as I knew him, even I had to look hard to see through his pretense.

Sitting on the couch in front of me, he put his drinks down and pulled my legs onto on his lap. My breath hitched in my throat as his hands began to trail down my thighs. There was something sexy and highly intimate about the way his hand moved slowly down my knee to my ankles. They lingered there, the warmth of his skin instantly arousing me. Despite Jett being one of the most successful businessmen, he had strong, capable hands. They were callused, which I knew were from driving fast cars.

"What are you doing?" I asked, my breath heavy.

"I promised you a massage. Did you think I'd forget?" He arched one of his sexy eyebrows and unfastened the sparkling gemstone buckles of my black high-heels. With a soft *thud*, they landed on the hardwood floor.

A second later, his hands were on me again, his thumb gliding softly across my skin. My body began to tingle all over. Deep inside, something began to pulsate. My breath caught in my throat again when his thumb glided sideways across my foot, and the gentle tingle was replaced by long, gliding strokes. My heart spluttered.

Boy, did I get it wrong. He isn't trying to help me relax, the little devil!

He was trying to turn me into butter with something supposedly innocent.

A massage? Really?

His smug smile made it obvious he knew exactly what he was doing. That worried me, because knowledge is power, and no man should ever have that kind of power over a woman—especially not over me.

"Where did you learn to touch like that?" I whispered.

He didn't answer at first. Instead, he turned his attention to my other foot. He wasn't just sinfully sexy; he had also mastered the art of entrancing a woman with nothing but the touch of his fingers. If he continued his torture, my brain would stop working. His massage wasn't just relaxing. Rather, it was as if the gates of heaven had opened, and my body became a liquid mess, pouring out of me, pooling around my feet.

"With you, it comes naturally," he finally said.

"I'm honored." I smiled, even though I didn't believe a word he said.

"Nothing's free though," he said, bemused. His green gaze met mine, and my heart jumped in my throat at the obvious insinuation. "And I know the perfect way for you to repay the favor."

For a moment, I was left speechless. My mind went blank, which was never a good sign. I wanted to be in control of my words, not the slave of green eyes and the deep rumble of a Southern accent, and especially not a slave of his magic hands.

Do I really want to play hard-to-get just so I don't have to admit my ridiculous weakness for him?

"Sure," I mumbled to myself.

When his grin widened, I realized I must've spoken out loud. With a devilish glint in his eyes, he whispered, "You surprise me. I had you pegged as the bargaining type."

"I didn't mean that."

"No, you didn't." His lips twitched.

"I'm serious," I said grimly, realizing he was making fun of me. "I was talking to myself."

"Sure." He raised his hands in mock surrender. "No need to be defensive about it." His thumb brushed my inner thigh. "We all make that mistake."

Heat scorched my cheeks and probably turned them bright red.

Damn my pale complexion!

I opened my mouth but stopped myself before I dug an even deeper hole when it was already too late.

"Whatever," I whispered. "We'll have to go over our terms before I sign the dotted line."

"Obviously." He arched his eyebrow, amused. He was so close I could barely breathe. His scent, his touch, and the dimples in his cheeks—they were all too much to handle. "So, Miss Stewart..." He paused for impact. "Tell me something personal about yourself. Something I don't know."

I flicked a stray strand of unruly hair out of my eyes as I considered my answer. His question took me by surprise. I didn't like talking about myself, because words were like gateways to the past. One wrong turn, and there would be no way back, so I carefully stuck to the basics. "I'm a real estate agent and project manager, working for an up-and-coming real estate company," I began warily. "I graduated two years ago—"

"I'm not interested in your résumé," he said, cutting me off. "This isn't a job interview, Miss Stewart. Right now, all I want is your body, so let's try again. In the bedroom, what's your favorite position? What do you love to do?"

I stared at him, stunned by the brash question. I hadn't quite expected him to be so bold. Eyeing him carefully, I moistened my lips.

"Does it have to be in the bedroom?"

His lips twitched again. "No. You can choose any place you like."

"If I could choose anywhere in the world, it would be near a fireplace." Unknowingly, my eyes focused on the fire next to us and on the soft rug spread across the hardwood floor. I didn't mean to be so honest or obvious, but for some reason, the cave of my mouth instantly turned dry at the naughty thoughts taking shape inside my head. A fireplace just so happened to be one of my fantasies, the kind of place I had always dreamed about. On some subconscious level, I had blurted it out because I wanted it to happen.

And Jett Mayfield was the perfect man to fulfill any fantasy.

"That's pretty tame. I thought it'd be somewhere public, like sex on the beach," he whispered in his low, irresistible

Southern drawl.

My cheeks heated again. "I'm not really into public displays of anything," I whispered, remembering the distinct feeling of embarrassment mixed with excitement. "There's always the risk of being caught."

He leaned forward, interested, his hands parting my knees just a little. "But you'd do it, wouldn't you? Just for the sake of saying you tried it. If you were given the opportunity, you'd go through with it?"

Where the heck was he going with this?

I tilted my head sideways, unsure of the hidden meaning behind his words. There was a promise, no doubt about it. A silent intention. Maybe even a plea. But the hotel room was as private as it could get, and it was too cold to do it outside, so his suggestion simply made no sense.

"Possibly." I shrugged. "But, like I said, the chance of being caught is way too high."

His sexy smile widened, almost as if he knew what his hidden promises were doing to my body. "What if I told you there's a way to do it without ever being caught?"

I let out a snort. "Right. Unless you have some kind of superpowers, like making us invisible and changing the weather, I don't know how that could be possible."

"I booked this place for a reason, Brooke."

Of course.

My pulse spiked from the way his sexy Southern accent

emphasized my name, caressing my nerve endings. He was as close as any person could get to a sex god. I fought for breath, completely aware of the sudden wetness between my legs, even though he hadn't done anything in particular other than massage my feet.

"What are you saying?" I whispered.

His gaze caught mine. "Let me show you something." His lips curled up at the corners. He let go of me and got up, towering over me.

I had no idea what he had in mind, but the mere suggestion of him doing something—anything to me— aroused me.

He held out his hand, and I placed my palm in his. My heart pumped hard as he pulled me up and led me to the grand piano near the large bay windows. At first, I thought it was to play on it, but when Jett stopped in front of the large bay windows, I sensed something else.

We were standing in front of the glass, high above the city, with nothing but the soft light of the fireplace illuminating the room behind us. The glass in front of us became an almost invisible barrier that gave the impression we were standing on a cloud. Stretched out in front of us were thousands of city lights, sparkling in the distance. Snow was falling in big white chunks, covering the city in white. It was beautiful, breathtaking. I had never seen scenery like that, at least not in real life. I wanted to comment on the beauty of New York, my hometown, but Jett shifted behind me.

His hand pulled my hair back gently, a motion so tender it made my heart beat a million times an hour. He slid aside the soft fabric of my dress, exposing my shoulder, and then his hot lips began to kiss my neck, causing the butterflies deep within me to flutter in a frenzy. His presence was overpowering, his kiss on my bare skin heating me from the core. My breath hitched in my throat. I opened my mouth, ready to implore him to do as he pleased, to take me in all the ways he wanted to, but that would have been too easy.

"You're sexy," he whispered in my ear. "I want to take you right here, right now."

I turned to face him and immediately regretted it. The sky was a moonless, black pit, but the lights of the city and the burning fire were enough to illuminate his face and those emerald eyes of his, metaphorically weakening my knees and my resolve.

Damn those sexy eyes.

Ever so slowly, his fingers trailed down my spine and began to lift up my dress. My blood pumped hard in anticipation as he tugged at the thin strings that held my panties in place. Under his knowing fingers, they came loose. Now I knew why he had demanded that I wear those for our little date: they were easy to lose in general and even easier to lose to a man like him.

"Is this your new idea of public sex?"

He held up my panties, dangling them on one finger. "You bet." Grinning, he tossed them behind him.

I watched them drop onto the floor, wondering what he had in mind.

What do you think, Stewart?

It didn't take a genius to figure it out. I only had to look at the sparkle in his eyes—the hint of his naughtiness and the promise of wild sex. As if sensing my thoughts, he flashed me his trademark panty-dropping smile. "Good thing I asked them to light a fire. Now we'll only have to make your little fantasies real."

Chapter 6

"AS YOU CAN see it's not quite public, but it's the best I could come up with without breaking the rules," he said.

"Sort of," I said. "People working in the other buildings can still see us." It was a half-hearted protest. I knew he could brush it off easily by telling me they were too far away or that no one was working in the neighboring skyscrapers at that hour, but he didn't.

"Probably," he said instead. Ever so slowly, he stepped closer to me and moved his hand around my waist, and then turned me around to face the city lights, my back pressed against his hard body. "They only have to look through their windows to see us." His voice sent a delicious shiver through me. "Imagine it, Miss Stewart. People might see us, but nobody will know who we are."

My heart hammered harder.

He wouldn't, would he?

Unfortunately, I could picture it too well, because he had a risk-taker look about him that screamed both trouble and danger.

"You're crazy," I whispered, barely able to utter the words.

"Thank you."

"It wasn't a compliment," I muttered.

"Well, I'll still take it as such."

His mouth lowered onto my shoulder, and his lips grazed my skin in countless slow but delicious kisses. Rolling my head back, I suppressed a low moan. As he started to unzip my dress from behind, the room began to spin slightly.

"We can't do this. Not here," I whispered.

"Who says we can't? It's perfectly legal."

Barely.

His hot lips nibbled on my ear, intensifying the gathering hotness between my legs. And then, all too quickly, his mouth took its leave. I turned in protest when his hand forced my dress down my hips. I watched the fabric gather around my ankles in a messy heap.

I was panty-less, my unmentionables covered by nothing but my bra and my hands. That certainly hadn't been the plan.

Legal wasn't good enough. I wanted *decent.*

"Well, in that case, forget what I said. I *can't* do it here." Even to me, the protest sounded feeble, the result of my weakness for him. In my mind, I knew I was taken—my love conquered and sealed. I just wasn't ready to admit the little fact to him.

"You wouldn't be standing here if you didn't want to," he whispered. "You know, that dress you wore was a good choice. All the time, I've been thinking about ripping it off of your hot, little body." He leaned in, and his lips found my skin again, kissing, sucking, and nibbling on me as he ignored my words.

I could feel him everywhere: on my neck, on my shoulders, each kiss so soft it brought on a new set of delight.

Sweet mercy!

I knew I had to protest. I wanted to, but it was too late. His fingers began to fumble with the hook of my bra, and eventually it came loose. I pressed my bra against my breasts before he could snatch it away. The lacy, silky fabric was the only thing that preserved my modesty, and I had no intention to let it go so easily. Even in the dim light of the fire, I couldn't allow my chest to be exposed to the whole world.

As if sensing my internal struggle, Jett laughed against

my skin and tugged at the stretchy fabric. When that didn't work, he tickled me. With a scream, I let go and spun around furiously, my hands wandering up to cover my naked breasts, but he beat me to it. His hands grabbed mine, and he pulled me against his hard body. "You're so cute when you're like this."

"Give it back," I said, demanding my bra.

He shook his head slowly. "You said you've never had a one-night stand. Before I booked this place, you assured me I'd be able to do whatever I want and this is what I want, Brooke. So play nice."

It was true.

While I knew he liked to test the boundaries, to see what made me tick, the truth was that I loved him being in control. His readiness to jump headfirst into adventure was infectious, but more than that, he knew how to send a wicked sensation through me and keep me hooked on his games.

But could I admit that to him?

Hell, no.

"Not a chance," I said, with enough determination to even fool myself.

"Shush." He pressed a finger to my lips and shook his head. "No talking. I'm going to give you what I promised—new things, new experiences, new sensations. All with me. But I won't force you. If you want this, you're going to have to ask." His fingers brushed softly over the core between my naked thighs. "And you have to ask...nicely."

"I won't," I said decisively.

He snorted. "Yes, you will."

"Try me." I lifted my head and stuck out my chin.

"I was hoping you'd say that." He laughed softly in my ear.

He raised my arms a little and commanded me to touch the glass. Pressing my hands against the cold surface, I held my breath in both anticipation and fear of what would come next.

He inched closer to me and spun me around until the front of him was pressed firmly against my back. Heat spread in every direction as his hands moved down my arms, slowly but surely, while he continued to kiss my neck, moving further down. Then, in one quick motion, he spread my legs.

Holy shit.

My breath caught in my throat.

His thumb began to rub my clit with an eagerness that would give me the blush of the week. I tried to fight him, at least in my mind. I really did, but my brain soon succumbed to his determination, and his thrusting became the source of both delicious pain and pure enjoyment coursing through me.

"You're so wet, baby," he whispered and dipped one

finger inside me while his thumb continued to circle my clit. When I moaned in response, he slid in a second finger, his movement becoming faster with each thrust. "I love knowing I'm the reason you're so turned on."

"Thanks, Captain Obvious," I whispered in mortification.

"No, really. You're doing a great job, Lady Hotass." He licked my earlobe. "You're about to get wetter."

Did he have to be so brutally honest all the time and point out the obvious? I swallowed down the embarrassment washing over me.

It was no secret that I was like an open book to him, too easy to read, a part of me wishing my body wouldn't give away the telltale signs of just how badly I wanted him. I felt ashamed, but the truth was: it didn't really matter—at least not *that much*. My desire was bigger than my wish to hide my weaknesses from him. My need for gratification mattered more than my plan to play hard-to-get. And, frankly, I didn't care if making out in front of a window was inappropriate because I felt as though I was exploding.

The glass under my hands felt cold, a welcome distraction from the heat inside me. With Jett behind me and my legs spread apart to accommodate the slow but persistent thrusting of his fingers, I leaned into him, nearing my release. The pressure was building, and soon I would fall apart.

"Please, Jett," I whispered at last, when I thought I couldn't bear it any longer.

Inside, I was vibrating. My body was trembling. I was ready for him. There was so much want—for his touch, for him—that I was ready to beg some more, just so he'd finally give me the release I desperately craved. I expected endless asking and shameless pleading, but he stopped before I could ask again, and he pulled his fingers out of me.

Ready to protest, I turned to face him. As our eyes connected, a stronger, deeper ache began to throb between my legs—the kind that just crashed on me. With shaky hands, I fumbled to unzip his pants, urging him to undress.

Sweet mercy.

He was horny and hard.

It was then that I realized just how much I wanted him, how willing I was to do whatever it would take to have him inside me.

Right now.

As if sensing my desire, he pushed me against the window. The cold glass caressed my feverish skin as his hot mouth descended upon me, kissing me hard.

"God, you smell so good. Are you even real?" he whispered as his hands cupped my ass. His hot tongue dipped into my mouth, intensifying the hotness and pulsating between my legs. "Not yet, baby," Jett whispered hoarsely.

But I had to have him inside me! I wasn't going to wait a second longer.

"I need you, Jett," I said, barely able to speak. "I want you...now." I wasn't just asking; I was pleading, begging him to take me.

Pressing my back against the glass, he entered me in one swift motion, pushing his entire length into me so fast that he almost made me come. I sucked in my lip as my sex welcomed his fast thrusts, each deeper than the previous, every one of them perfect, as if he and I were strung together as one musical instrument.

Throbbing heat gathered in my core. I tensed in a futile attempt to prolong my pleasure, but it was too late for more. Between his fast moves, his quick breathing, the pulsing and rubbing inside, my being shattered, and I came undone. Distantly, I heard his deep, sexy moan. I felt his moisture spilling inside me, and a smile lit up my lips at how perfect that moment was.

Chapter 7

WE WERE LYING on the couch, my chin resting against his chest. The soft glow of the fireplace illuminated the room, turning our naked skin into a game of light and shadows.

We'd performed three different sex positions in less than an hour, a number that wasn't bad at all. We had done it against the window and the piano, and finally in front of the fireplace. To claim I was exhausted would have been an understatement; my core was still throbbing. I felt free, fulfilled, lost in the euphoric aftermath of my climax—a part of me wishing time would stop, holding us captive in that afterglow forever.

So, when he stirred and got up, I propped myself on my

elbows, confused.

"Just stay put until I get back."

I frowned. "Why?"

"I need to do something. It won't take long."

I looked at him, my curiosity instantly piqued. "Okay."

He gave me a short kiss, and then he was gone.

With a shrug, I leaned back, pondering what could be so important that I couldn't go with him. By the time he returned, I had squeezed back into my black dress. There was no sense in running around naked.

"Ready?" he asked, flashing unnaturally white teeth.

I eyed him suspiciously. Something was going on, but I couldn't figure out what it was. It was too late to ask anyway, because his hand settled on my back, nudging me to walk ahead of him. When we entered the dining room, my breath caught in my throat. Jett had lit candles and scattered rose petals on the hardwood floor.

"I got us dessert," he said, his voice giving away a hint of uncharacteristic nervousness.

I turned to him in surprise, only to find his dark green eyes boring into me. He was so beautiful that it broke my heart.

Scratch beautiful!

He looked like he could steal one's soul with just a glance and get away with it.

Maybe it was the intoxicating scent of the candles, or

maybe the way Jett kept watching me full of anticipation, but in that instant a strange thought entered my head—completely unrelated, and partly frightening:

Oh, my god. Is he going to propose?

It couldn't be. Not Jett, not here. Or could it be?

My breath hitched in my throat again and my heart started to race as I narrowed my eyes, *really* looking at him, my mind simultaneously ticking boxes:

I was pregnant. Check. And we had something really good going on. Check. His suggestion to spend the night at one of the most expensive hotels had come out of the blue, and what a night it had been. Jett had told me he was in love with me weeks ago. So was that it, the big moment?

Is he that serious? And will I say yes? Can I? Should I?

My head was spinning. He had stolen my heart and soul to make me his. It would only be fair to steal his last name and make him mine. Slowly, I brushed my hair out of my face and curved my lips into a dazzling, encouraging smile. Then, all of a sudden, I was overcome with fear. I didn't know how I'd react if he asked the question, but I sure knew the answer.

"What?" he asked me, sensing my nervousness. A dimple appeared on his face.

"Nothing. It's just beautiful here," I whispered and almost choked on my own thoughts.

What if he asked me? Would I really say yes?

Hell, yeah, I would.

In the blink of an eye, with no hesitation, no fear.

Thoughts continued to swirl around in my head, but I didn't have to ask myself, to consider, to decide. I knew I wanted to marry him. Jett was so sexy and so bad that he was good. Plus, he could drive a car like he stole it.

What woman in her right mind would refuse a ring from him, no matter how small the stone? Definitely not me.

I groaned inwardly at my own weakness for him and promised myself that, if he asked me, if it ever happened, I'd force myself to pause. I would just hesitate for a tiny bit. Under no circumstances would I jump into his arms or scream with joy, saying yes over and over again, God knows how many times. I wouldn't act like those silly girls in the movies, nor do anything that would make me sound too desperate. At twenty-three, I wasn't desperate; I refused to be.

No, I would act like a reasonable, elegant, and mature woman. I would nod, smile tenderly, act utterly surprised or maybe even shocked. I would say, "Are you sure?" or "Wait, is this a proposal?" and then answer in one word, "yes", and dab my eyes with Kleenex to make sure my mascara wouldn't smudge.

I wouldn't choke and squeal. I wouldn't cry and certainly not scream. Nor would I grin like a fool.

Oh my God, how wonderful would it be if he proposed?

I squealed inwardly at the mere thought, but it was true. In every way, Jett was perfect. He was like the shore kissing the ocean, like facing the setting sun. I was blinded by him and taken in by his glory.

Asking for my hand in marriage would be a dream come true. It would be an assurance that I'd always be the only woman in his life. Because, whether I wanted it or not, Jett was the man for me.

As we sat down, my heart gave a little shudder, and I brushed my hair back in the hopes of accentuating my features. If Jett was about to propose, where was he hiding the ring? I eyed the dark chocolate mousse, decorated with roasted nuts, and hoped he hadn't chosen to hide it inside the dessert; I didn't want to do anything stupid like choking on a bite or a diamond. There was nothing particularly attractive about the Heimlich maneuver or about turning pale and blue while scaring your lover to death during what was supposed to be a special moment.

"I thought we could have some romantic dessert," Jett said, jerking me out of my thoughts.

I looked up to meet his clouded gaze. His expression was serious, his eyes were misty, his mind elsewhere.

And then his phone rang, but he didn't seem to notice.

"Don't you want to pick that up?" I asked.

He looked at the caller ID, then quickly stuffed the phone back in his pocket.

"It can wait." His tone darkened, mirroring the suddenly cold glint in his eyes.

Wow.

It had to be important, and he didn't want to ruin or cut short our weekend together. Otherwise, why would he have brushed it off so briskly? I eyed him closely and couldn't help thinking how complicated sometimes men were, changing from one extreme to another. I wanted to press the issue, since his mood seemed to have taken a complete nosedive into gloominess, but he cut me off before I could bring it up.

"Let's eat," Jett said coldly.

I peered at the dessert and took a bite. In spite of the rich chocolate color and hefty price tag, which probably gave away the hotel's quality when it came to food, the mousse stuck to the back of my throat, and I could barely swallow it. It was hardly how I would have imagined a marriage proposal to go.

That's because it isn't one, Stewart! my inner cynic cried, causing my heart to sink in my chest.

No proposal, then. I tried to stifle a disappointed sigh...without much success.

"I'm glad I didn't let you go when you broke up with me the first time," Jett said, completely oblivious to my dismay.

"What makes you say that?" I asked and frowned, thinking back to the first time we met. We had fought; we had loved, and then came the betrayal that eventually brought us back together and made us stronger than before.

"I was just thinking about the circumstances that led to our breakup." He looked back at me with an intensity that rendered me speechless. "When you walked away the first time, I thought about you every minute of the day, wishing I could turn back time and meet you under different circumstances." He paused slightly, as though to choose his words carefully. "It made me realize how sorry I was for hurting you, and how differently I should have and could have handled that situation."

I remembered that day too well, because it was the first time someone broke my heart. Back then, after dating him for three weeks, I found out I had inherited a multi-million dollar estate in Italy, and Jett had targeted me because he wanted that property. Eventually, I allowed him to explain his motives, and I even forgave him for not being honest with me right from the beginning. Even though opening up to him and letting him back into my heart had been hard, I had been willing to give him a second chance.

So far, I hadn't regretted that decision, but I'd have been lying to myself if I claimed I had forgotten all about it or the feelings of betrayal it caused me. Or the realization of just how embarrassingly gullible I once was. It would have been all too easy for things to turn out differently; for instance, he could have easily used me for his own selfish motives rather than to save his father's company, Mayfield Realties.

"It happened a long time ago." I looked away so he wouldn't see the hurt in my eyes. Truth was, yes, it all happened a long time ago, but while time could heal all wounds, this one had gone a little deeper than the rest.

"Yes, but..." Jett took a deep breath, taking his time to finish his thought.

I couldn't help but wonder why he'd risk bringing up such a heavy topic after having such a good time, but I remained quiet as I waited for him to continue.

"You slipped away, Brooke, and I realized that even the darkest moments in my life before you entered it were nothing compared to not knowing whether I'd see you again." He looked up and something passed over his features; it was the same ominous glint I had seen before, like dark clouds gathering before a thunderstorm.

"We broke up, we made up, and now you have me again." Keeping my tone light, I shrugged. I didn't want to think of *that* topic or *that* time. The mere mention of our breakup and the consequent prospect of an empty future— a future without him—had rendered me hopeless. Just thinking about it made me sad, and this wasn't the time nor the place for sadness. "You explained your motives, and I chose to believe you."

"I know. It's just...well, I wish it never happened," Jett

said softly. "But at least it made me realize you're the risk I'll always take."

I frowned. For some reason, the statement—the odd combination of words—annoyed me. It wasn't just the prospect of him taking risks for me; it was the way he said it.

Big words.

Yeah, that was the problem. Big words too easily spoken. So easy it was hard to believe them. Words weren't always easy to prove, and I certainly would never expect him to. While I had no doubt that he meant his statement, I didn't want to *hear* it. I *knew* Jett would stand by me, no matter what. After all, he had saved my life when I was in trouble, even though he could just as well have turned his back on me.

But talking about the risks he'd take for me?

It was like an invitation not to live up to expectations. It was like an invitation to hurt me all over again. One thing my past had taught me was that big words equaled false promises, resulting in disappointment, and I had more than enough of that already.

"We'll be there for you, honey," people had promised at my sister's funeral, and again when my father died. Then, in the weeks and months that followed, not one of them showed up to check on my mother and me to see if we were coping. In some ways, that was worse than not saying anything at

all. I would've preferred a quick hand squeeze or a soft smile as long as the moment lasted, because at least that would have left us with the impression—even a prospect or a false belief—that the pain in people's eyes was heartfelt, that we weren't just an inconvenience, never to be thought of again.

Better forgotten.

I balled my hands to fists. As much as I loved hearing Jett's words, I wanted him to show me the sincerity of his words later, maybe in a few years' time, when life had settled and there were no more mysteries left, when novelty became monotony and routine, and maybe even tragedy. Years later, when he would be able to say with full confidence, *"She was always the risk I'd take. I knew it right from the beginning."*

Right now, however, relying on his words just wasn't an option for me, even if I wanted it to be. I had to be prepared to be loved and left. To be hurt again.

Because *that* was reality.

Life was beautiful, but it was also painful. People fail, a few get up, but there's never a guarantee that their second attempt will work out. Claiming I was the risk he'd always take when he didn't know what the future would hold in store for us was just wrong.

Too wrong.

"The future is an endless pit of uncertainty and

promises, some of which might not come true," I said, keeping the rest to myself. "There's no point in talking about risks or decisions, Jett."

Talking challenges fate. It attracts disaster and causes chaos to unfold.

"I know what's true for me, and what I'd be willing to do for you," he said stubbornly. An angry undertone was palpable in his voice. He propped up on one elbow and turned to glare at me. I ignored the two lines that had formed between his brows and took a long, deep breath, ready to stand my ground.

"I understand, but there are so many bad things that could happen."

"Nothing bad will happen. I won't allow it." His gaze met mine with such ferocity that I had to swallow past the sudden lump in my throat. He was dead serious, and his intensity scared me.

A guy like him could love fiercely and drop it all in the blink of an eye, just as fiercely. A guy like him could also walk blindly into the fire, ignoring the smoke that was about to kill him. Didn't he realize that just because we loved each other and would soon have a child, life never comes with an assurance policy? *We* might not last—no matter how deeply we loved each other right *now*.

"Maybe," I whispered.

His glance hardened just a little more. "Brooke," he said,

in a tone that left no room for discussion, "I'm serious. I would do anything for you, no questions asked."

My jaw clamped shut, unwilling to continue so as not to annoy him even more, but I wasn't going to budge on the subject either, and he knew it. Besides, Jett would probably come up with countless reasons when I didn't want to listen to any of them because, deep in my heart, I knew Fate always had a few surprises up her sleeve. It was a lesson I'd learned early on in life. But how could I possibly explain to him that even if his ego would never admit it, Fate always called the final shot?

"What, Brooke?" Jett asked.

"You wouldn't understand," I said.

"Try me."

I shook my head, realizing that dropping the subject was the best way to go. Even if I explained myself a thousand times over, we'd never see eye to eye. We were too different and yet alike, and that was the perfect recipe for disagreements and fights.

"I don't want to," I said. "In fact, I don't want to talk anymore."

"All right. I guess the conversation's over." Without waiting for an answer, Jett headed out the door, calling over his shoulder, "I'm taking a shower."

No invitation to join him.

I set my jaw and slumped into the cushions, not

bothering with a reply, the aftertaste of the chocolate mousse leaving a sour taste in my mouth.

Chapter 8

I SHOULD HAVE just waited for Jett to finish his shower and join me, but something prompted me to get up and open his laptop. Just to check my emails, not to go through his stuff. He did it all the time, so I didn't understand why I had a sudden feeling of foreboding in the pit of my stomach.

I opened a private browser and navigated to my email account, then typed in my details. There were at least fifty unread messages, most from work, some from friends and acquaintances—nothing important enough to demand an immediate reply. I skimmed through all of them and decided to log off, but before I did, I clicked on the recycle bin, curious as to what was residing in that little trash can icon.

The message was there, marked as read and deleted. It had been sent from a prominent legal firm in New York City, the kind of firm that tended to be in the news on a weekly basis. With a fleeting glance at the door to make sure Jett was still in the shower, I opened the message. I blinked several times in succession, for a long moment unable to process what I was reading:

Dear Miss Stewart,

We're contacting you on behalf of a client who is interested in acquiring the Lucazzone estate, which we have reason to believe is in your possession now. Our client has had the estate appraised by an independent third party and would like to discuss with you an offer that would benefit both you and your future plans. You may contact us during office hours at the number below. I can also be reached on my private line at your convenience...

My heart began to slam against my chest in big quakes that rendered breathing impossible. I read the first part again, then moved on to the less important stuff, which included their company letterhead and some legal wording marking the email as private and confidential. Hundreds of questions raced through my mind, all demanding attention at once. Who was the mysterious client? And how did the legal firm get a hold of my personal email address? How had they known I was the heiress to some old estate that harbored dark secrets?

I shook my head and took a deep, shaky breath as I forced myself to focus on one question at a time. But my brain couldn't move on from two basic facts. First, someone was interested in purchasing a multimillion-dollar estate that belonged to me. Less than six months ago, as an estate agent, I would have been thrilled to arrange such a deal. It would have been an amazing opportunity—the big chance, for both my career and my financial status. Then again, less than six months ago, I had no idea I'd inherit the property the moment Alessandro Lucazzone died. Which led me to point number two: someone had logged into my email account and deleted the email on purpose. And why hadn't the firm contacted me at work to talk with me directly? Unless my calls were being screened.

I knew the message could be spam, sent from some hacker who might have found out details about me and decided to target me in a scam. But for some inexplicable reason, I decided to believe it was the real deal. The correspondence details looked too professional. The legal firm was well established in New York City business circles. Given the fact that a private number was included, I figured the request might be either urgent or important, so I memorized the number and decided I'd call it as soon as possible.

Somewhere in the periphery of my mind, I realized that the sound of running water had stopped. Jett must have finished his shower and would be joining me any minute. I hurried to log off and close the Internet browser, then placed the laptop back on the table and returned to my previous position, all while my mind continued to fight against the onset of mistrust that was quickly nestling inside me.

"Hey," Jett said from the door, a towel wrapped around his naked lower body, "why didn't you join me?" His spirits had risen, and a smile had returned to his lips. Slowly, he inched closer with the kind of hooded look that screamed sex—and lots of it.

"You should dry off before you flood the floor." Forcing a smile to my lips, I pointed to his hair and crossed my arms over my chest.

He got the hint instantly, because he didn't come closer. Instead, he headed for the bedroom, presumably to get a change of clothes.

I exhaled in relief. At some point I would have to ask him about the email, but now wasn't the right time. I was too shaken and needed time to think about the estate and the future the email had mentioned—a future that now included a child.

Chapter 9

JETT RETURNED WITHIN a few minutes, dressed in a white shirt that accentuated his broad chest and narrow waist. Under different circumstances, I would have insisted on ripping it off of him, but now my attention was focused elsewhere.

"Are you okay?" Jett asked. "You seem a little distracted."

For a moment, I pondered whether to ask him about the email.

And risk sounding insecure? No way!

"I have a headache," I whispered. At least it was the truth.

"I hope it has nothing to do with what we discussed

earlier." He stepped closer, wearing a concerned look on his face.

"No, that's not it. I'm fine." My voice came a little too high, betraying my lie.

Jett sighed. "Look, Brooke, I know you want me to shut up, but we need to talk about the future. Or else it will eat you up. Pretending you're fine when you're not is not the solution."

Playing for time, I sat up and tucked my legs under me, knowing I had to tread carefully so I wouldn't hurt him or start a fight. "Let's leave the past in the past and the future in the future." My voice came a little too defensive and strong. I cleared my throat, but didn't quite manage to get rid of the serious edge. "The future's not really something I want to focus on right now."

A silence ensued, the heavy and gloomy kind, like fog draped around the room. Except for the soft crackling of the burning logs and the rhythmical ticking of a clock, no sounds broke through the magnitude of the situation.

Finally, Jett got up and walked over to the table. His back was turned to me as he poured himself a glass of double-malt whiskey. The stronger kind—I noticed—which he only drank when something troubled him. I knew how much he actually disliked whiskey. He swigged it down in three gulps and winced, then poured himself another and some water for me.

The tenseness of his shoulders gave away his anger at my unwillingness to explain. And I understood: he wanted me to share with him everything, and I would...someday. But right now, for the time being, my past, my fears, and my thoughts were my business. They were my burden—a closed door I wasn't ready to open.

Jett put the glass of water on the side table.

I wrapped my fingers around it, but in spite of the dry sensation in my mouth, I didn't drink any.

He gave another frustrated sigh and moistened his lips. "Brooke, I'm just saying..." He paused. There was something in his voice that made me look up. Was it hesitation? Caginess? I wasn't sure, but I could feel something in his stance, some kind of alertness, as though he was carefully watching my reaction. "I'd never do anything to betray your trust. I'm always going to keep my promises to you, but you need to trust me."

I frowned again.

I hated the word "trust." It reminded me of a house of glass that allowed everyone to enter freely or see what was going on inside. Eventually, someone would want to probe that glass and see how far they could go without breaking it. Maybe even go as far as damaging it beyond repair. People never talked about trust unless there was a good reason. More often than not, there was a morbid curiosity behind it, a hidden motive or an agenda— sometimes good, sometimes bad, however we saw it. That was just the way it worked. So, how could he stand there and talk to me about trust when I had just found the email in the trash and was plagued by burning questions?

Narrowing my eyes, I took in the burning intensity in his gaze. He wanted something from me, but as much as I wanted him to elaborate, a more urgent question kept burning on the tip of my tongue.

"I don't understand. Why did you bring up our separation earlier?" I asked, trying to keep the tone light…without much success. "Why would you talk about risks?"

He took his time with an answer. Finally, he drained the last drop of his drink and looked up. "Because I don't want it to ever happen again." There was a slight pause, and then he continued, "It's not so much about the risks I'd take for you, but it's more the fact that I want you by my side, no matter what happens. We can fight. You can scream at me. Hell, you can even punch me, but I need you to stay, *no matter what,*" Jett said slowly. "I need your promise that you won't disappear like before."

I shook my head and frowned again. "I'm afraid I don't understand."

"It's simple, Brooke. I'm asking you to promise me that you won't leave."

My heart skipped a beat, and a chill ran down my spine.

It wasn't quite the answer I had been hoping for, more like...*Look, I checked your email. I deleted it. And yes, let's get married.*

Not *that* answer.

I moistened my lips, hesitating. The way he was looking at me—too composed, too determined—made me nervous.

A promise that I'll never leave?

How could I promise that? What if he hurt me again? While I didn't fear the fights, I wasn't sure I would survive another crack in my fragile heart.

My fingers reached for the flickering candle on the side table—an old habit born out of pain and a need for control—and for a moment, I remembered the feeling of being burned. There had been a time when I welcomed the sting and the painful blisters. Just like a flame, Jett's actions had once burned me. He had shattered what we built over days and weeks, after which came the claim that, even back then, he had loved me.

He was my flickering candle—so beautiful yet so dangerous to the touch. Promising him that I would trust him, that I'd never go away, was like lighting a match and waiting for the flame to singe my heart and soul. I wasn't yet ready to surrender all control to him. For the time being, I needed to belong to myself.

"I can't, Jett." I shook my head, just in case he didn't hear my whisper. "I just can't." My gaze remained glued to my hands, my knuckles white under the taut skin. "I'm sorry."

The silence was oppressing. No, make it upsetting. Utterly, totally depressing. For a long time, it remained unbroken and suffocating, with no reply.

When I couldn't take it anymore, I gathered the courage to look up, only to see the dark glint in his eyes. There was a depth in them that spoke of chaos and secrets, of wanting to possess and not quite knowing when to let go. Or maybe it was the chaos inside me that I saw reflected in his eyes.

"Why not?" he asked eventually.

It was just a question: no pressure, no blaming. It was a simple inquiry, as if he was asking why I wouldn't want to take the rest of the day off work.

Why not actually?

Because it's not him. It's you. You can't trust him.

Despair washed over me as I realized it wasn't just a question of whether or not I wanted to trust Jett. It was a matter of whether I would even be able to trust him. Just as some people lose the ability to laugh or be happy, trust no longer came naturally to me. And while Jett seemed perfect in every way, after discovering that email, I felt a strong need to find out whether I could trust him. After all, there had been a time when Jett had targeted me for my estate...and that I would never forget.

Was it all just some odd coincidence that the email was

deleted? Or was it maybe some sort of sign?

I wasn't sure.

"Letting you back into my life was hard for me," I whispered. "You've taught me what it means to love, but life's shown me how easy it is to lose it all in the blink of an eye. That scar might fade over time, but it'll never go away. If I make such a promise, I'll basically be giving you my permission to hurt me all over again, just because you'll know I'd never leave. And I'm not going to do that, Jett. I can't, and you shouldn't expect me to. There's no way I'd ever want to repeat the experience of loving and having my trust betrayed."

He leaned forward, his expression hard and unreadable. "Are you saying you won't make a promise out of fear that something might happen to us? Between us?"

"Yeah, something like that." I let out a slow breath. A cold chill washed over me as I thought back to my parents. Unconsciously, I pulled my legs up to my chest and wrapped my arms around them while my thoughts about the past slowly shaped into words. "My father made a promise to my mother. I still remember how much he loved her." I paused for effect. "But in spite of his deep love and his vows, when my sister died, none of that was enough. He still left her. He killed himself, betraying his own vows, his promises, and breaking my mother's heart. Even to this day, she hasn't recovered from that blow."

I looked up and realized that Jett was staring at me, hanging on my every word, but that wasn't the only thing I saw before my eyes. The picture flickering before me was that of my parents fighting over me, because I had let my sister sneak out, on the very night when she met her tragic fate. Her boyfriend, Danny, had sold her like a prostitute.

"My father didn't love my mom enough not to leave her behind, nor did he find it in his heart to forgive me," I whispered, unable to stop a tear running down my cheek. "That was enough proof to me that love and life are unpredictable, just like a storm. So…" I looked up to meet Jett's beautiful, green gaze. "I don't want you talking about risks, Jett—or trust, for that matter. Life is unpredictable, and the circumstances of today might not be the circumstances of tomorrow."

He touched my hand gently, but not imposing. "This is different, Brooke. What we have is different."

I shook my head, pressing my lips into a tight line. The difference didn't matter; it didn't matter how different what he thought we had was. In the end, there would only be one outcome, one finale. It could end well or badly—a simple conclusion with absolutely no guarantee.

"I want a choice, Jett. An option," I whispered. "I want to be able to leave if you betray me or lie to me again. I can't promise you that I'll stay. What I can promise, though, is that when we fight, I'll listen to your reasons, and then make up my mind. But I won't give up my choice to leave."

"That's not good enough," he said, his jaw clenching.

"I'm sorry, but it's the best I can do."

"It's still not good enough. I need you to stay so I can protect you." He placed his hands on my womb. I gazed up at him, my whole body tensing. Something shifted in him, and I realized that I had taken it all wrong. It wasn't just about our separation; it was a matter of life and death. He was concerned because of the things that had happened back in Italy and New York. I closed my eyes to escape the memories that flooded my mind: being abducted and locked up, a young woman's brutal rape, and the knowledge that I'd be next. That was my life before now.

"Now that you're carrying my child, I have a right to make the decisions, and I say you'll never leave my side again," he said, as though reading my mind. "I don't want anything bad happening to you or our baby."

I sighed, blinking back the tears. He knew too much about me, and that in turn made it impossible for me to escape my memories when I was around him. It was hard to believe that he'd delete that email, but no one else, not even Jett, had access to my account. Still, he had the means to log into my account by using his connections. He was asking me to trust him, yet he'd done something so untrustworthy already.

"Look, I understand that you're worried," I said, "but—

"

"No buts." He shook his head, his eyes never leaving mine as he interrupted me. "I don't think you understand, Brooke. I'd kill for you and our kid. Being without you for so long, living with that fear of not seeing you again, taught me that nothing's more important."

"Don't say that."

"But it's true."

I bit my lip hard and turned away to escape the stubborn air wafting from him. Still, even without looking at him, I could feel his determination. My head began to throb. I didn't want to think about anything. I didn't want to remember. If only I could press a button that would erase parts of my memory, I would. It wasn't just the pictures flooding my mind that scared me; it was also the feelings of despair and hopelessness stemming from the knowledge that there was no escape in sight, burning bright inside my heart. In my dreams, the ropes that held me bound still cut into my skin. I had tried, but stopping the pain from haunting me seemed impossible.

"Let's talk about this another time," I whispered, shivering in my dress. "Please."

I wrapped a blanket around myself, got up, and walked to the bay windows.

Jett followed me and wrapped his arms around me, pulling me against him in silence. There was something calming about the snowflakes falling from the sky—an assurance that life would go on, no matter what happened; an assurance that I wasn't so different from others. Somewhere, somehow, someone had suffered just like me, and they had survived. A survivor is living proof that with each day, each year, memories weaken and gradually become a distant fragment of the past. I needed that hope.

"For what it's worth, I'll never let you go," he whispered in my ear, "even if you can't give me the promise I want."

I smiled bitterly. The heart is a castle of glass. Sometimes we're tempted to invite someone in, not to see them stumbling upon our deepest secrets, but to see if they care enough not to break it. Maybe one day I'd give him the key, but not before I saw if he cared enough about me.

Chapter 10

LOOKING AT JETT reminded me how much I adored every part of his body and mind. We were so much alike in character and spirit, and yet we weren't. The tiny crinkles around his eyes showed how much he loved to laugh. The soft line on his forehead hinted at his tendency to worry even when he tried not to show it. Just like me, he tried to hide his emotions, but there were signs that gave him away.

Unlike me, however, he didn't deny the obvious when confronted with his demons. Unlike me, he didn't run when things turned out to be more complicated than anticipated. Everything he did and said served a purpose, which was why I had to find out if he had logged into my account and deleted that email or, worse yet, contacted the legal firm. I figured it was time to get my answers; if I didn't, the questions would haunt me forever.

I eyed the door, then the dress I was wearing. I still looked like a stripper, but this was my chance, probably the only one I would have today. I had to hurry. There was no time to change.

"Is it bad that I want you again?" I asked and turned to take in Jett's expression.

He let out a deep, throaty laugh. "I thought you'd never ask."

His lips found mine, and as he kissed me deeply, the walls around me slowly began to crumble. I was his. Promise or not, he had claimed me. Now I just had to find out if he was my gloomy doom or my bright joy, because I had no intention of accepting anything gray in between.

I pushed him back. "You had your fun. It's my turn now." I escaped his grip and began to walk to our bedroom, beckoning to him to follow me.

And Jett did, helpless to my swaying hips, his eyes sparkling with naughty thoughts. Soon, the door closed behind him, and we were alone. I switched on the bedside lamps. His clothes were draped on the back of a chair, along with his belt.

If my plan was to work, I had to be convincing and conniving. I grabbed the belt, then turned around, new confidence spilling over inside me.

"Lie down." My voice was self-assured and commanding, leaving no room for disagreement. When he didn't comply, I pushed him down onto the bed.

He looked up, surprised, and his lips curled into a wicked smile as he eyed the belt in my hand. "Are you planning on playing badass?"

"You have no idea." My smile matched his as I pulled his hands over his head and bound them to the bedpost. Loose enough for him to wriggle around. Tight enough so he couldn't leave.

If Jett thought it was too tight, he didn't let me know.

Thank God, the penthouse beds had bedposts; otherwise, I would have been forced to bind him to the chair and make love on the hard floor. The idea of what I was about to do brought a giggle to my lips, but Jett didn't notice. His gaze was completely held hostage by my short dress—or more precisely, what was under it. I rewarded him for his compliance by gliding my body along his, letting my breasts rub against his hardness, just the way he loved it. I had to do whatever it took to arouse him and make him surrender to my will.

My fingers grabbed his slacks and pulled them down his hips. A moan escaped his lips as his erection jerked out, its size both fascinating and terrifying, its slick crown velvety and ready to unlock the most primitive of feelings inside me. He looked so impressive and beautiful, I could barely breathe as my fingers ran down his swollen shaft, marveling at his hardness.

Leaning against his hard body, I took a deep breath and smiled as his manly scent registered within my mind; nothing in my life had ever smelled so good. I inhaled the scent of his earthy aftershave and him—rich, smooth, edible, so mouthwateringly sexy that I wanted to take a bite of him.

Soon...but not now.

Pleasure had to wait, because my little act had little to do with sex. I needed more from him now than an orgasm.

"You're so hot that we need ice," I whispered against his ear. "In fact, let me get some from downstairs. I'll be back in a minute.

"We have an ice machine." He sounded so desperate and eager that I had to stifle another giggle.

"Are you telling me what to do?" I arched a brow in mock annoyance. "Mr. Mayfield, let me remind you that you're bound and entirely at my mercy."

"Now that sounds scary," Jett said, still grinning.

"It is. If I were you, I'd take it seriously." I stood and threw a sensual glance back at him. "If you behave, you'll be rewarded with something sexy. Now play nice, and shut up until I get back."

His grin widened until dimples appeared. "Yes, ma'am."

I closed the door behind me. It had been so much fun to bind him like that, when he was unsuspecting and trusting. The image of leaving Jett waiting the whole night and facing his wrath in the morning was so amusing that I snorted with laughter. I should have done something like this a long time ago.

I retrieved the phone from my handbag and the keycard from the coffee table, then hurried down to the reception area, where I was sure Jett wouldn't look for me, even if he somehow managed to untie himself because he couldn't bear not being in control.

The night-shift receptionist barely looked up as I passed him. Time to move to the next step in my plan. I hid in the corner and dialed the number I had memorized. As I waited, my heart slammed hard against my ribs, so hard I was sure it was going to give out on me.

"Damn," I murmured under my breath when the call went straight to voicemail. Sighing, I tried one more time, still without success.

Maybe their battery was dead? Or maybe they switched their phone off, because they were sleeping, which was understandable, since it was eleven p.m. Either way, I decided to call them one last time and leave a short message, a request to call me back during office hours. It wasn't ideal, but I could rest in the knowledge that I had done all I could for the time being.

Eventually, I returned to the receptionist, an older man. He eyed me in a friendly way as I explained that I had no idea how the ice machine upstairs worked. He just nodded patiently, obviously used to being bombarded with strange requests at night. I waited patiently as he brought me a champagne bucket filled with ice cubes.

"Anything else I can help you with?" he asked, flashing those unnaturally bright teeth that were typical of New York City employees.

"No, that will be all. Thank you." Giving him my best smile, I took the bucket and headed back to the elevators, ready to commence my torture on Jett.

The elevator doors had almost closed when a hand slid in to stop them. When they opened again, a man stepped inside. He was dressed in an old-fashioned suit, and his hair was combed back. I realized he was the same man I'd seen lurking around the lobby earlier that day, and he was still carrying a newspaper.

"Good evening, ma'am," he mumbled, barely looking at me as the doors closed.

Alarm bells began to ring in my head, and my heart thudded impossibly hard, hammering against my rib cage the way it always did when I found myself alone in a closed space, with someone I didn't trust.

"What floor?" I asked, trying not to sound too uneasy.

"Twelfth, please." Rather than looking up at me, he

nonchalantly unfolded his newspaper and began to read it again.

I pressed the elevator buttons a few times too many, and stepped back, holding my breath.

The guy cleared his throat, but his gaze remained glued to the newspaper.

Please go faster, I urged the lift. I wasn't sure what made me think that, but there was something about the man that scared me. Maybe it was the way he dressed, austere and old-fashioned. I had no idea.

It was then that my glance fell on the newspaper. There was nothing special about the article he was reading, something related to sports, but it was the date that caught my attention.

The newspaper was three days old.

How odd!

My pulse doubled in speed and began beating a furious staccato. Naturally, I tried to slow down my heart's frantic pounding, but my hands wouldn't stop shaking.

The lift finally stopped on the twelfth floor with a *ding,* and without saying another word or glancing back at me, the man left.

When the door closed behind him, I was able to relax. It wasn't in my nature to judge other people's behavior, but the guy was just creepy. I shrugged inwardly. So what if he read an outdated paper? Many people did, didn't they? It had probably been lying around and he had picked it up, reading out of boredom. Maybe he was an avid reader, eager to devour each word he came across, or maybe he'd been out of town a few days and wanted to catch up. They were all perfectly reasonable and rational explanations. But for some reason, my heart continued to slam hard within me. It was only after I returned to the safety of our penthouse that I could calm down, and my thoughts returned to Jett, who was still bound to our bed, the email long forgotten.

Chapter 11

THE NEXT MORNING, I woke up alone. Soft sunrays streamed through the high bay windows, illuminating the gold and cashew hues of the bedroom. I turned to peer at Jett's empty side, my fingers touching the soft material of the bed sheets. The silk still smelled of him.

Of us.

Of our lovemaking.

Stroking the smooth surface conjured memories of him touching me, and my whole body began to ache again. I smiled. Only Jett could take me the way he had, and set my world on fire.

While I loved his enthusiasm when we were together and loved everything about him in general, I wasn't so keen on his whole early-dawn routine, and he knew it. For the umpteenth time, I wished he'd taken the time to wake me up before taking off, instead of leaving me alone in a huge, empty bed.

I was vaguely aware of what had happened between us, of that promise he had asked for. It didn't take me long to realize that my refusal to give it to him might have been the very reason why he had left. Maybe he was trying to piss me off by keeping me waiting, or maybe he intended to punish me by making me think he could sneak out whenever he wanted. He wouldn't do that, though, would he? Surely he wouldn't be so conniving. Or maybe he was off somewhere, checking my email.

"Right," I murmured to myself as a pang of anger shot through me. I wasn't going to give him that promise, at least not yet. He had to earn my trust, and if he could be stubborn, so could I, if not more so. I was going to find out the truth soon enough anyway.

Rubbing my eyes to get rid of the tiredness, I sat up and turned to grab my phone from the nightstand, ready to dial the legal firm, when I noticed it was gone.

I frowned, immediately forcing my mind into action.

I had left a message on the Wighton & Harley's answering machine with a request to call me back in the hope they would bother to get in touch with me. That was the reason why I'd wanted to keep my phone near me in case they tried to reach me. Then there was Sylvie. She had texted me the day before, and I had meant to read her message. I distinctly remembered leaving my phone on the nightstand, right before I joined Jett in the bedroom.

So, where was my phone?

Wrapping the sheets to cover my naked body in a makeshift toga, I stood and walked over to rummage through my handbag, near the windows on Jett's side. When I heard steps in the hall, I stopped in my tracks.

I knew the footsteps were his, slow and steady, as if he knew where he was going and what he was doing. Just like everything else he did, Jett's steps were always as if he poured his whole energy into every minute of his life. And now, he was heading toward our closed bedroom door behind which I was standing.

My stomach lurched. What if Jett had been here the whole time, somewhere in that huge penthouse, and I panicked for no reason? Even if that was the case, I couldn't afford to let him know it.

First of all, I didn't want to appear desperate. That was definitely a no-no.

Second, I didn't want him to think I didn't have a life of my own, which would have been worse than appearing desperate.

I ran back to the bed, unsure if I should pretend to be still asleep or twist myself into a sexy pose.

I snorted at the thought: I couldn't act or pose seductively even if I wanted to. My acting skills sucked. They were even worse than my cooking—an ability that was practically non-existent because I was certainly no culinary genius. All things considered, I decided it was best to try to look as if I had just woken up.

Yeah, that could work. I'll stretch my arms over my head, do some head-rolls, and let out a hearty yawn.

I nodded, pleased with my own plan, and readied myself to slide over from his side to mine...only, too late.

The door opened, and Jett walked in with an amused look on his face as he regarded me. I swallowed, and not because he had just caught me in an awkward position—on all fours, with my butt pointed right at him. Wearing a black jacket, a tight, gray shirt, and sexy jeans that perfectly accentuated his broad shoulders and narrow waist, he looked so badass that I could have ripped his clothes right off his body. No matter how much I wanted to, I couldn't think of anything to say.

He was pure sexiness, and my body reacted to him like he was made of honey. In every sense, he was all I could focus on. His body, his eyes, his voice: it was as if he had been made to be glorified.

"Like what you see?" Jett asked, drawing my attention back to his face.

I rolled my eyes, cursing the fact that I was so weak for

him. He was my very own addiction. I decided the only way to cure my body's weakness for him was to deny that he had that kind of effect on me.

"It requires a little more to impress me," I said dryly. "I'm not all about muscles and a pretty face, you know."

Amusement glittered in his eyes as he curved his lips up in a sexy smile. "That's a shame, Miss Stewart. You strike me as a meat person."

I opened my mouth to hit back with a snarky remark, but then he pointed to the trolley behind him, which I hadn't noticed before. It took me a few seconds to realize the meaning of his words: he was talking about breakfast. And a big one at that. I stared at the carted feast in disbelief.

Holy crap.

Had Jett decided to raid the hotel's kitchen?

There were so many things to choose from, enough to cater to a small party, and make you feel like an idiot for not being able to name each food. My stomach churned as my eyes scanned the delicious-looking pastries and bagels, and the smoked salmon arranged around a vast selection of bacon and cheese, granola, and fresh-squeezed orange juice. A folded newspaper was arranged next to a narrow vase that held a single red rose. I stared in awe, barely able to contain my delight. I had never seen an omelet with lobster claws, and was that caviar? There was even a bowl full of strange-looking exotic fruits, some I'd never seen before.

Talk about a variety worthy of a royal visit!

Unwillingly, I peeled my eyes off the breakfast tray and turned my attention back to Jett. "Is this all for us?"

"It's part of the penthouse package," he said. Pressing a sheet against my chest, I followed him into the living room and watched him as he grabbed a fork and frowned. "They didn't include the Alma caviar though when they should have."

"Really? How rude." My voice matched his disapproving tone, though I was unsure whether he was seriously complaining about fish eggs or just joking.

"Gold caviar sells for thousands of dollars. I wanted to know if the price reflects the quality," he continued, not taking the hint, and dipped a fork into the black layer covering half the omelet. "Let's hope the alternative is as good as they claim it is."

Holy dang!

He had paid thousands for some slimy, black goop that barely looked edible? Or was gold caviar made of gold? If it was, I could probably sell a spoonful of the stuff and pay my month's rent, and still have spare change left. Mortified, I looked at the caviar omelet, not sure whether to laugh or be shocked. Was food even allowed to be that expensive? The idea that people would spend so much on a few morsels was beyond me. And frankly, fish eggs? Weren't they like little fish droppings? I stared at the fork he was holding and realized they certainly looked the part.

"Try it, Brooke."

"Do I have to?" I tried to suppress a scowl but failed. I had never really had a thing for caviar. I had tasted it once—probably the fake stuff—and found it disgusting.

"You'll like it." His voice was barely more than a whisper, but there was enough force in it to convince me that he wouldn't take 'no' for an answer.

Taking a bite, I forced myself to chew slowly, and leaned back, surprised. It tasted delicious, reminding me of the sea, with just a hint of lobster, olive oil, and herbs.

"Not bad."

"See?" Laughing, he heaped some on the fork again and held it up to my lips.

Maybe it was the baby talking, but I suddenly felt ravenous. I wanted to take another bite when Jett stepped in front of me—too close not to think about sex—and I noticed his lopsided smile.

"I wouldn't skimp on this either." His voice came low and hoarse.

Confused, I looked up at him, with no idea of what he was referring to. But there was no need to ask. His gaze dipped slowly from my eyes to my lips, finally settling on my breasts. As I looked down, I noticed that the covers had shifted, revealing more than was decent. Heat blushed my cheeks, and I quickly pulled up the sheet in a weak attempt to hide some of my skin. He stopped my hand before I could cover myself.

"I don't like you covered up." He grinned. "In fact, you're so sexy that you shouldn't wear anything at all."

"I can't do that," I said, shocked at his preposterous suggestion.

"Of course you can. In fact, as long as we stay here, I must insist that you run around naked."

I felt myself blushing even harder, probably turning a shade of crimson, as his hands pulled away the remaining fabric, exposing my body, naked from head to toe.

Under his green, burning gaze, my body behaved as though it belonged to him, as if my soul had been touched and marked, and I just had to react whenever he was near. His hands stroked my shoulder, the gentle touch raising the hairs on my arm in anticipation. Slowly, his mouth dipped onto my skin, and his hot lips began to send delicious currents down my back.

I leaned back, savoring his presence, until something cold brushed my neck. When I looked down, I noticed something sparkling. In his hand was the most beautiful necklace I had ever seen, a tiny stone dangling from a delicate chain. Even though the diamond was cut in a round shape, its mount was the form of a heart. I gasped in surprise, marveling at its beauty.

"I hope you like it," he whispered. "I got it for you while you were asleep." Jett clasped it around my neck, then brushed my long hair aside. "When I saw it, I had to get it. I knew it would look perfect on you."

"Thank you." My heart hammered hard as he pulled me in front of a mirror and stepped behind me. For a few moments, I gazed at the small gemstone, marveling at the way it seemed to enhance my collarbone. It was so small, so simple, yet it was so stunning that I could only stare. The more I looked at it, the more I was convinced that it had been expensive. Jett never went for the affordable stuff.

"I understand that you can't make any promises," Jett said. "I have to admit, I don't like that, but I want you to know that, like this diamond, what we have is rare and there's nothing I would change about you. Don't ever forget that, Brooke."

I touched the stone and slowly turned around, my voice failing me at the intensity in his green eyes.

"It's beautiful," I whispered at last.

"Not as beautiful as are you," Jett said.

I smiled tenderly, my pulse racing at the various thoughts spinning inside my head. We had gone through so much in the short period we had been together, but I simply wasn't ready for the kind of assurance he expected of me.

"You shouldn't have, Jett. It's lovely, but…I can't accept

this gift." I lifted my arms to remove the necklace when Jett's much stronger hand stopped me.

"You have to. It's what I want." He paused, his gaze broody and dark. "You are mine, Brooke, and I want you to have nice things."

He kept looking at me with an intensity that made my heart flutter. I wanted to say so much more, to utter my thanks, my gratitude, anything to show him that I valued everything he'd done for me, when his fingertips brushed my lips and his mouth descended upon mine.

In that instant, I realized something meaningful: words were futile. It's said people spend their entire life thinking about love, searching for it, thinking they have found it. But there is no word that can express the magnitude of feeling love, of having one's heart bursting with it at a mere smile. It wasn't just Jett's presence or his kindness that reached surreal proportions, but the fact that he reciprocated my feelings and that he tried so hard to express the way he felt. He really tried, as if his spoken words were true, as if he truly meant them, and he wanted to see me happy.

Ever so slowly, his mouth descended upon mine in a tender kiss. I wrapped my arms around his neck and pulled him on top of me, my legs parting to accommodate his weight. Jett didn't seem to need a wordy invitation. His tongue brushed past my lips to explore the cave of my mouth.

Pinpoints of rapturous sensations traveled down my spine and gathered between my legs. I needed him down there more than I needed the air to breathe and I was ready to show him.

I could have lingered in his embrace, lips on lips, forever, were it not for the knock on the door that drew our attention back to the world, to reality. When he let go of me, I realized that moment was lost forever, like a dream.

Chapter 12

MY HEART WAS beating a million times a minute from our kiss, and my body was still aching for him as I caught Jett's reaction. I tried to read the thoughts he kept so well hidden, but I failed for the umpteenth time.

"Who is it?" I asked, my voice low and thick with wariness. I hoped it was just someone knocking on the wrong door so we could get back to making out—anything that would distract Jett from his way-too-intense concentration.

"Probably just the butler. There's one assigned to every penthouse. Let me check," Jett said. He let out an impatient sigh, and then kissed the top of my head. "I'll be back in a second." Without waiting for my reply, he crossed the living room in a few long strides and closed the door behind him.

I turned to the mirror to stare at my reflection, unsure of what to do. I hated waiting, especially since the day had started out so perfectly, with Jett at my side, his strong arms on my thighs as we kissed on those silk sheets, and then his beautiful gift. The whole scene had been more than perfect, which is why I could forgive the small interruption—as long as he hurried to get back to me.

Wearing a goofy smile, I resumed my seat on the sofa. As I did, I noticed Jett's cell phone peering out of his jacket pocket, its screen illuminated with an incoming call or text message.

For a moment, I considered pulling it out to answer it, in case it was important. The fact that Jett had switched off the sound only managed to fortify my idea of Jett as perfect boyfriend material. Obviously he didn't want to know of any calls when he was with me.

How many other guys had done that for me?

None.

Precisely.

In today's society, where phones were often regarded as essential for survival, Jett was in the minority. He wasn't afraid to face total isolation with me, because he had no need for distraction. His attention was all mine. The thought of that made me warm all over.

Leaning back against the soft cushions, I tried to ignore

the flashing, but as the screen continued to light up, worry slowly set it. What if it was one of the company board members, who was trying to get in touch with Jett, because the stock was crashing and no one could get a hold of us?

Jett happened to be the owner of a newly formed company called Townsend Properties, but as the son of one of the most prominent men in the United States, he also still acted as the CEO of Mayfield Realties, which in the last weeks had survived a series of scandals involving an international sex club. Against all odds, Jett had saved his father's company from bankruptcy, all while focusing on his new company, killing two birds with one stone and making a name for himself. Some claimed the sex scandal was nothing but a marketing strategy to have the Mayfield name plastered across newspapers worldwide in order to attract attention to Jett's new company, Townsend Properties. Others didn't care. Only a few people, me included, knew the true secrets of what had really taken place in that sex club and the depravity of some of its famous members, who had chaired the Mayfield Realties board. I was the only one who knew how hard it had been for Jett to repair the mess and how difficult it had been to stop thinking about vengeance where he thought vengeance was due. After weeks of hard work to reform the old company and kick-start the new one, Jett wanted to focus more on our relationship, which was one of the reasons he insisted that we spent quality time together. Knowing he still had a job to do whilst on "vacation" with me, I couldn't just ignore the real world.

Without wasting another second, I retrieved the phone and peered at the screen. An unknown number had called numerous times, meaning it probably *was* important and Jett would have to call them back. Ready to dash after him, I picked up the phone and started to walk when my fingers brushed the envelope sign by mistake. The text message popped up instantly, and I couldn't help but read it:

The meeting will be no problem. Consider it done. TI

As I stared at the message my cheeks caught fire, and instant shame burned through me for snooping around when it was clearly just a confirmation text.

Talk about invading his privacy. How creepy or needy can you get, Stewart?

"Shit," I mumbled as I flicked through the phone settings for a button that might revert the text back to "unread." There was none.

Instead, another, earlier message popped open.

The setting is fine. Where exactly do we meet? Ground floor or outside? TI

Damn those freaking small buttons! Damn my clumsy fingers! Why had no one thought of inventing an application that double-checked if you actually wanted to read a message? Something that asked you to confirm it before it opened like:

"Are you sure you want to read this message? Click here to confirm."

Then:

"Last chance to avoid clicking this message and risk looking like a control freak."

Or something like that. And what kind of message was that, by the way? How hard could it be to show a little politeness by adding more words, like, "Hello? How are you? Sorry, I know it's your day off, Mr. Mayfield, but I just wanted to let you know that the meeting you required will take place. Thanks. Have a nice day."

Some people were so uncommunicative it probably pained them to talk. Then again, it didn't surprise me. Jett himself was as monosyllabic as one could get, so I figured the people who worked for him might just be inclined to pick up his bad habits.

In the distance, a door slammed, and sure enough, Jett's

footsteps thudded down the hall. He was coming. I looked around in a panic.

Crap!

How was I supposed to explain to my boyfriend, who just so happened to be my boss as well, that I accidentally read his text messages without sounding like I had some major control issues? Would he even believe me? There was no way I could revert the message back to unread, and I wasn't sure what to do. Should I delete it or just confess? Why did I have the feeling that telling the truth wouldn't help me? If Jett thought I was snooping through his personal stuff, there was a possibility that our day would end in a fight.

Scratch that.

Knowing Jett and his alpha male tendencies, I was actually pretty *sure* of that. It didn't even matter if he was the one who had logged into my email account seeing that I had no proof nor had I heard back from the legal firm.

Women's magazines always said that men couldn't stand women with trust issues. At present, we had not yet built enough trust to the extent I was confident enough Jett would look kindly upon me going through his phone. That, combined with the fact that he was my boss, had me worried that our relationship might just be over if he found out.

Without thinking, I pushed the phone back into the

pocket of his jacket in the hope another text might arrive in the meantime and Jett wouldn't notice that the previous one had already been read. I stormed out of the room, almost bumping into my surprised boyfriend as I headed for the one place where he wouldn't see my shaking hands: the bathroom.

Thank God, whoever invented it.

I closed the door, and sat down on the toilet seat, willing my heartbeat to calm down. At least I wouldn't have to come up with a good excuse as to why I had almost run him over, because nobody in his right mind would bother to ask a pregnant woman that. And if he did, I'd just say that, yes, I had to visit the restroom what seemed like a hundred times a day. If that didn't throw him off the trail, I could always blame my crazy hormones for making me act strange. And if even that wouldn't work, I could play my ace in the hole. I could accuse him of deleting my email, and brace myself for a fight, knowing that I'd lose that argument. After all, it would be hard to prove it had been him who logged on since I never gave him my password. But Jett had friends who could hack into anyone's private business if he so much as asked them for a favor, without anyone ever finding the connection. I had to take that into account, too.

But as things currently stood, I wasn't going to point the finger at him without having at least some solid proof.

***

Jett looked distant when I returned. His tight gray shirt was gone, replaced by a tailored business suit, white shirt, and a dark blue, silk tie. I stared at him, and instant worry set in. He looked like he was getting ready to leave—again. I wondered if he'd read the text message? And, more importantly, I wondered if he was pissed at me, if he had discovered that I had read it?

"I'm sorry," he said when he noticed me standing in the doorway. "I know I promised you an entire weekend, but I have to run some errands."

"Why? What's wrong?" I sat down beside him and intertwined my fingers in my lap.

"Nothing major, I hope. The service personnel knocked to let me know I received a call from the Trump building. They said it's urgent." He barely looked up as he arranged his cufflinks. "Some idiot messed up a contract and now I have to run back to the office and get his work done for a job that was supposed to have gone through last week."

"Can you not send John?" I asked, referring to his new assistant, a guy who had worked in the field for years. "Surely he can take care of this. You don't have to do everything yourself, you know." I smiled, even though it wasn't a joke. Jett had the tendency to want to take care of every detail, no matter how trivial.

"I'm afraid not."

I raised my brows. "Why not?"

"He's getting married." Jett smirked. "Which is foolish of him, if you ask me, because it's going to ruin his career. In my opinion, no one should get married, not until they've been dating for at least five years. It takes that long to get to know somebody. I have no idea why he's doing it. It's, simply put, a stupid move."

Got the point, loud and clear.

My heart gave an almighty *thud* as I stared at him.

No marriage, then.

I didn't know what was worse: that my hopes of getting married anytime soon were completely unrealistic or that I had thought that Jett was different from the rest of the male population.

Apparently not so much.

"Oh." I bit my lip hard as I considered my options. The weekend was ruined anyway, so I figured I might as well get back to work myself. "Do you want me to come along and help you? We could be done in no time."

He shook his head slowly and looked up. "That's not necessary, baby. Besides, this has all been paid for. You may as well stay here. I'd rather you enjoy yourself and check out whenever you're ready. Stay another day. You've worked too much lately and need to rest."

And by that he meant our unborn child needed to rest. For some reason, I couldn't stop more disappointment washing over me. It wasn't at all what I had hoped to hear. Spending a day in a luxury hotel and making use of all its amenities sounded delightful, but it wasn't the same without Jett or without being engaged. This day was supposed to be ours. Our time. Not mine alone, coupled with a strong feeling that I was single.

"How long will you be gone?" I couldn't help but ask.

"I don't know." Jett retrieved his phone from his jacket and began texting furiously. His face didn't change as he checked his messages.

I expected to be relieved, but the relief never came. Everything had started out so well, and now we were back to square one—the usual lack of conversation whenever Jett was in work mode. I could have that with the hotel personnel, or with any other person out there.

I pointed at the tray with food. "So I guess you're not having breakfast with me before you go."

"Brooke…" Sensing my irritation, Jett inched closer and cupped my face. "I know it's not ideal, and trust me when I tell you I feel like a jerk. But this is important." He lifted my chin until his green gaze met mine. "I promise I'll make up for lost time when I get back."

Knowing that any arguing would be pointless, I simply nodded.

"Great," I said, trying to keep my voice strong. "Don't worry about me. I'm sure I can find lots of ways to keep myself busy around here." I had no idea what came over me to make me sound so bitchy. Maybe it was the fact that life kept him so busy, and I missed that kind of independence and freedom—the feeling of being needed and wanted. Of being able to dive right into my work without being held back by a relationship or the promise of not letting anything get in the way of a romantic weekend.

"Thanks," Jett said and left, seemingly distracted. I sighed and turned around to look out the high bay windows, admiring the stunning view. It was only then that I glimpsed my phone on the piano.

I frowned.

It must have been sitting on the lacquered surface all along, even though I couldn't remember leaving it there. I grabbed it and slumped onto the sofa to check my calls. Still nothing from the legal firm, which was understandable. Companies as large as Wighton & Harley needed time to reply. I'd just have to be patient until they got back to me.

Meanwhile, I began to flick through my text messages. The last one was from Sylvie. I became awfully aware that I had been neglecting my best friend ever since I had begun dating Jett. We never had daily coffee meetings or afternoon shopping excursions anymore. The thought that I had put Sylvie on the back burner for Jett made me feel guilty. Sure, relationships required a constant input of work and attention, but so did friendships. At the moment, Sylvie was about the only person, who knew how to turn a gray, cloudy day into bright sunshine.

Sitting up, I began to text, ready to make up for lost time.

Chapter 13

IT WAS A done deal. After a few text messages, I managed to persuade my best friend to take a break from work and meet me at a bistro near Central Park: my suggestion, my plan.

When Jett left after a hurried and awkward breakfast, I took a quick shower and returned to the forgotten suitcases in the hall, the ones we hadn't yet had a chance to unpack. As I tried to open mine, I realized it was locked, and the key was nowhere to be found in my handbag.

Had I absent-mindedly left it at home? Lost it on the way here? I stared at my suitcase in shock as realization slowly dawned on me: my clothes were in there. Without them, I had little choice but to go either naked or dressed like a stripper.

Think, Stewart. Wear yesterday's clothes and walk around in a tight dress in the middle of a day?

Hell, no.

It wasn't just the strange looks I was worried about, but Sylvie's huge dose of sarcasm and several rounds of ridiculous interrogations.

I was in no mood to have to explain Jett's kinky attempts at keeping the spark alive in our relationship. And especially not, when Sylvie was as curious as a cat.

I checked the time. If I hurried, I could make it to Jett's apartment and back on time before my coffee date with Sylvie…sort of. I figured I might just be a tiny bit late. An hour at the most. Or I could just keep the meeting brief and pretend I didn't want to take off my coat. Or that I dressed like this every day now.

Why the heck do you even need to explain, Stewart?

Sylvie wasn't one to judge. If anything, she would probably applaud me for embracing what she would call my "inner sexy lioness."

With a nervous smile, I shrugged back into my tight dress and coat. A last glance in the huge mirror of the elevator and one more brief attempt to arrange the soft, brown ringlets of my dark hair into a half-decent twist, and I walked out.

Either it was the half-empty lobby or the fact that my

initial excitement had somewhat dampened a bit, but something felt different. Unsure what it was, my glance swept over the creamy marble floors and the water fountain in the middle of the hall, and came to rest on the man standing in the exact same spot as before, a newspaper still clasped in his hand.

I swallowed past the lump in my throat.

Just as before, his hair was combed to one side in a sleek, flawless style, as if he felt a need to convey an appearance of perfection. He was dressed in a business suit that had seen better days. On closer inspection, I noticed it was actually the same business suit he'd been wearing earlier—blue with stripes, a loose-hanging cut, as if it was a couple of sizes too big for him. He was alone this time, and there was no sight of the woman who had accompanied him on the previous occasion.

Forcing my legs to take measured steps forward, I hurried to the door, my heart beating hard for no particular reason.

My reaction made no sense because I didn't know this man. And yet the mere sight of him—that particular memory of the way he had looked at me the day and night before in the elevator—was enough to send a chill down my spine.

But it didn't matter. As I passed him by, he remained engrossed in the article he was reading and didn't look up.

He didn't even react when an elderly woman entered, obnoxiously dressed in furs, carrying a mini-schnauzer in her large bag. Even when the yappy little dog let out an ear-piercing bark, the man did not flinch.

I, on the other hand, jumped, suddenly aware of the squeaky canine and the way the noise seemed to carry, lingering in the air.

Calm the fuck down, Stewart.

Ignoring my own advice, I peered around me in a panic. People turned their heads to glare in the woman's direction. Everyone seemed on alert, disturbed by the sound, and several seemed annoyed that the woman could not control her pet—everyone but the mysterious guy with the newspaper. He was the only one who wasn't unnerved by it.

I stared at him and frowned.

He didn't seem the least bit perturbed by the woman or her dog. He just continued reading, entirely unaffected or perhaps unaware. His unnatural focus irked me and raised my suspicion.

My pulse spiked, and my heart began to slam just a bit harder against my rib cage.

Calm down. It's just an irrational reaction in a harmless situation.

My therapist had once declared that I had the unnerving tendency to feel things that weren't there, things that didn't even exist. "That's just your anxiety talking," he had said, "and those irrational fears will create doubt." It was one of the reasons why I couldn't trust people. Still, the knowledge didn't stop the unease wreaking havoc inside me.

Wrapping the coat tighter around my waist, I dashed out the door and headed for the small bistro at the end of the street, ignoring the curious glances cast my way. No one seemed to be running, and the fact that I was probably made me look like a fugitive on the run in this part of New York City.

It was barely eleven a.m., and although the autumn air had filled with a chilly wind, the snow had stopped falling sometime during the night. Judging from the dark November clouds and the way the weather changed constantly, it looked like the snow was going to be replaced by rain.

I stepped into the small bistro. The warm air inside was more than welcome. In the far east corner of the open space, I spotted Sylvie. She had already taken her preferred spot, next to an oversized potted plant and the window overlooking the busy street. Her head was bowed over her smartphone, her fingers sliding over the touch screen while she texted. I had no idea how she did it, but her appearance was more flawless than ever. Even on the worst of her days, she looked as if she was about to enter a beauty contest. With her tan complexion, blonde hair, and blue eyes that resembled the deep Southern sky on a summer day, she would have won the first place.

She looked like an angel in disguise, sent from heaven above. I had no doubt that if anyone tried to cause me any harm Sylvie would jump right into the action and take a bullet for me. As long as there was no robbery or a creepy neighbor involved, she was in every way fearless, and no one would want to mess with her. The knowledge that I knew my best friend so well brought new tears to my eyes.

You're being emotional, Stewart.

Damn right, my hormones were raging again, slowly turning me into either a rampant psycho or a crying heap, whose waterworks might just start flowing at the mere sight of a baby seal. I couldn't wait for the pregnancy to be over and done with, if only to let me regain some of my emotional balance.

As I headed for Sylvie, her eyes caught mine, but her smile quickly turned into a look of suspicion. I couldn't stop the tiny tremble from running down my spine. She had been my best friend for a long time. As such, she knew everything about me, including the ugly past I was still trying to forget. The way she seemed to look right through me, I felt vulnerable and exposed. I figured if Sylvie were an android, her eyes would be like X-rays, able to penetrate the deepest layers of tissue and discover all the things better left buried forever.

I shrugged out of my coat and draped it over a chair,

then sat down.

"Nice, Brooke." Sylvie nodded appreciatively as she pointed at my dress.

No point in lying.

"It was Jett's idea," I said. "I borrowed it from your wardrobe."

"He has a good taste. I'll give him that." Grinning, she hugged me and kissed me on both cheeks. "How was your night at the TRIO?"

And the inquisition was beginning…now.

I watched her lean forward. "And don't leave out any details. I want to hear it all."

Did I have to? I shook my head. At times, I wished she didn't know so much about my life. It was a futile wish, an energy wasted, because Sylvie was as intense as a hurricane and had the iron will of a bulldog, mixed with the sixth sense of a hawk. Intuition came naturally to her. For all I knew, she might be psychic. Having no choice, I began carefully, "It was beautiful. Jett was very attentive, as usual."

Sylvie smirked and waved at me, a gesture intended to dig a little deeper.

Absent-mindedly, I scanned the small bistro as I prepared my words. Apart from the two of us and an elderly couple sitting close to the entrance, there were no other patrons. I watched the way the old man's hand rested naturally on the old lady's as they talked in an animated fashion, as if they still had a lot to talk about, even after so many years. They were having a good time, just like Jett and I had before the disruption and before he revealed his views on marriage. Above Sylvie's head, a huge heart painting hung on the wall. It seemed that no matter where I looked, I was reminded of love and Jett, and of the hours that were stolen from us. The day had started as ours, and I wished it had stayed that way.

"Whoa. You look weird. Did something happen?" Sylvie's excited voice drew my attention back to her. "Did he propose? You know, whatever happened, I should be the first to know, because I'm your best friend, right?" she said with a wink. "I'll be seriously pissed if I find out that you've been keeping secrets from me."

I winced.

Her words stung. It wasn't so much that Sylvie would think I'd actually break our girls' code and keep a secret, but the fact that what I had been hoping for didn't happen. When Jett had declared that he'd booked a weekend for us, I'd convinced myself it would be capped off with a ring on my finger—or at least a request to put one there. He'd been talking about a future together, and I was sure he was ready to make a big commitment. When Jett didn't propose, I realized, quite painfully, that it had been nothing but wishful thinking on my part.

"Why would he propose, Sylvie?" I snapped, a little

harsher than I intended. "Just because a man books a hotel doesn't mean he's ready to pop the question."

I knew I sounded defensive, but for the life of me, I couldn't keep the bitterness from tainting my voice. "Jett's rich and successful. Of course he's not planning to tie the knot anytime soon. At least not in this early stage in our relationship."

"Sorry," Sylvie said softly. "I was just asking."

I was such a hypocrite for trying to make her feel bad when the very same thought had kept me glued to Jett's every word and watching his every move. For days, I'd been waiting, expecting, hoping. Reminding myself of how much I had changed.

Less than a year earlier, I had been the one who didn't believe in commitment, and marriage had certainly not featured anywhere in my life plans. Now, for the first time, with Jett by my side, I wanted more. His generosity and big words when it came to our relationship weren't enough to prove to me that what we had was real. I had to have him near me, with me forever—written in black and white—and not just as the father of our unborn child.

"It's okay," I mumbled, avoiding my bestie's probing gaze.

"I'm really sorry." Sylvie spread her hands, palms up. If my tone had offended her, she did her best not to show it. "All I'm trying to say is that I wouldn't have been surprised if he had asked. I mean, you guys seem to be getting pretty serious. Plus, you're pregnant, and you're already living together, so..." She left the rest unspoken, hanging heavily in the air.

I stared at her, unsure of what she was getting at.

Why did she make it sound as if Jett's proposal was long overdue?

We were serious, weren't we?

But...

There had been the odd weekend when Jett insisted we spent time in expensive hotels, always together. Even though we hadn't been told the baby's gender yet, there had been talks about names, how she or he would be raised, and what school our child would go to.

So, why did it feel like something was missing?

As I pondered, I clasped my hands together, breaking out in a sweat.

And then it hit me like lightning.

Once. Twice.

We had made plenty of short-term plans but, thinking back, I realized there had been no conversations about our future as a family, about the three of us: Jett and I and the baby. No plans as to where we would be living after the child was born. Just big words about our undying love and his support, but there had never been any specific talks of a nursery or what would happen after I gave birth.

Nil. Nada. Zip.

Jett's two-level penthouse apartment was spacious, but with its architectural design, including an open staircase, dangerous railings, and floor-to-ceiling windows, it was too unsafe and in no way the right place to raise a child.

Dismay washed over me at the thought that I had absolutely no clue what the future held in store for Jett and me. Of course, my best friend would ask if he had proposed. She had every reason to be concerned. I might be blind in love, but Sylvie was as objective as a bystander, which was why I figured I should be listening to her.

"I'm sorry." I released a deep, shaky breath that I didn't even know I'd been holding. "I didn't mean to snap at you."

"Don't worry about it." She waved her hand dismissively, completely unfazed. "It happens to the best of us."

"Let's order," I said in a cheery tone that was quite contrary to the turmoil swirling within me. I waved a barista over and asked for two cappuccinos, and then turned my attention back to Sylvie.

She was still staring at me, her blue eyes betraying her concern. "What's going on?" she asked quietly.

I pressed my lips into a tight line. Finally, I leaned back, unsure of how much I could reveal without tugging at my heartstrings.

"I don't blame you for asking. I asked myself, too," I admitted slowly. "The fireplace and the champagne, along with the fact that he booked the most expensive suite—a penthouse—made me think he was going to propose. He had this beautiful dessert sent up, and rose petals strewn all over the floor...well, it would have been the perfect moment. It really was." I trailed off, reminiscing about our time together, unable to suppress the sadness and disappointment nagging at the back of my mind.

"Oh, sweetie." Her hand clasped around mine, squeezing gently.

I shrugged as if it didn't matter, even though it did. "But instead of asking for my hand in marriage, he demanded that I promise not to run away, not even if we separated in the future. As if such a promise would be enough to keep our relationship going for years." I paused as I remembered his words. Five years, to be more precise. "Needless to say, I couldn't do it. I just couldn't make that kind of promise."

I looked up and almost began to laugh at the way Sylvie's eyebrows furrowed. Wrinkles didn't suit her. They made her seem stern, and she didn't do stern very well.

"Why?"

I moistened my lips. "If I make a promise without getting a promise back, I'll always think that he's not as invested in the relationship as I am. It makes sense not to give in to his every demand."

"So you didn't do it?" she asked, incredulous, and I realized she wasn't on my side. "The guy is crazy about you, and he wants the reassurance that you won't run away."

I shook my head, slightly irritated by her response. "You don't understand. I can't."

"What's the big deal? Just do it or pretend to. It's probably only a matter of time until you two get hitched anyway."

"Not for the next five years, we're not." I grimaced. Just thinking about his words made me feel defeated.

"Why's that?"

"Jett implied that marriage is for the foolish, and…" I waved my head as my words choked me. When the barista brought us our cappuccinos, I plastered a fake smile on my face to hide my emotions.

"He said that to you? Just like that?" Sylvie leaned back in shock.

"Not directly, no." I shook my head again and watched the barista depart. "He pointed out that he feels it takes that long to get to know someone, so I don't expect a marriage will happen anytime soon. But…" I looked up, ignoring the aching burn in my heart as I considered my words.

"But what?" Sylvie prodded impatiently.

I let out a frustrated sigh, then pretended to take a sip of the hot beverage, when all I wanted was the warmth to comfort my cold hands. The cup took the chill out of my fingers, but the warmth didn't reach the freezing sensation settling around my heart. "I'm pregnant...and to be honest, I can't really wait that long. Call me old-fashioned, but I need more. I need some sort of assurance that we'll last. A little more proof that we're in it for the long haul and not just for fun."

I eyed the liquid in my cup. Before I met Jett, my life had been dark in so many ways: impenetrable. Unforeseeable. Always filled with the need to stay awake, out of fear that my nightmares might just become real. Now things were different, and I couldn't help but wonder how my life would turn out if he ever left. Because a breakup was a possibility, what with my body changing in the coming months and the child demanding all of our attention. And even if he still found me attractive after I gained too much baby weight in all the wrong places, what if the years would pass us by and Jett continued to shy away from any sort of official commitment? Where would that leave me?

"You could propose to him, you know," Sylvie suggested. "Many women do it nowadays. All we'd need is a ring."

I snorted.

Granted, it wouldn't have been a bad idea...under different circumstances. Maybe if I were dating a guy who didn't mean so much to me. But I would never propose to someone like Jett, because a rejection from him would break my heart.

"It'd be pointless," I mumbled. "He's had more women than he can count."

"So? He has you now. Who cares about before?"

"Well, I do," I whispered. "It just proves that someone like him doesn't commit easily. He said his past doesn't matter, that I'm the exception, the only woman he's ever loved."

"Sounds romantic," Sylvie cut in.

"Sounds like bullshit, coming from someone who doesn't like to be tied down." When Sylvie inclined her head, clearly unconvinced, I continued, "Did it ever occur to you that he might only be asking for that absurd promise because I'm pregnant and he just wants the child in his life?"

For a second, we stared at each other in silence.

It was only when Sylvie's gaze fell on the necklace that I remembered how much Jett cared for me. He did his best to make me happy. Just because he had his personal views on official, legal commitment, it shouldn't matter if he and I got married or not, as long as we stayed together. I suddenly realized I was being too harsh on him. Instinctively, I touched the pendant, and guilt washed over me for wanting so much of him when he already did more than anyone had ever done before.

"I'm sorry," I whispered in a feeble attempt to conceal my inner thoughts. "I shouldn't think of him that way. He's trying so hard to make it work that I have no right to judge him."

Sylvie grabbed my hand again. "It doesn't matter. It's how you feel. And I totally get you, Brooke." Her voice came so low that I wasn't sure I heard her right.

"You do?" I asked, surprised.

"Yes. In some crazy way, I do." Sylvie smiled and squeezed my hand again. "It's your right to have wishes and dreams. We all have them. It's what makes us who we are—susceptible, stupid, and blind. But love gives us hope to live another day."

That was why I loved Sylvie. She never judged me, but more importantly, she understood where I was coming from—at least most of the time.

"I'm not really an expert in relationships. You, of all people, should know that," Sylvie said. That was true. She was anything but a relationship guru. In fact, she usually shied away from them like the plague.

"But I know this. Marriage is not such a big deal," she continued. "People think that once they're married, problems won't ever arise, but the truth is, there's always work to be done, marriage license or not. Two people can be married and still not be committed to each other. But then two people can be committed and happy without having to be married. My point is…you don't need a ring to prove that your love is real, because marriage doesn't give your relationship a day off work. It doesn't make it easier or give you the happiness you should find within yourself."

"So, what do you advise?"

She hesitated before she proceeded warily. "Since Jett's your first real relationship, I say you should throw caution out the window. Just go with it, and stop being overcautious."

"Great." I sucked in my lower lip. "I'm overcautious, and he's overprotective. What a perfect combination."

"Better a careful combination than nothing at all," she said. "At least Jett wants to know how you are and what you do."

Was that bitterness talking?

Her tone made me look up, and something passed between us. It was just a moment, but it was enough to know what that look meant.

"Has Kenny called?" I asked, treading carefully.

"I wish." Sylvie smirked. "But it's not the end of the month yet, so he might decide to."

I nodded encouragingly as I tried to conjure Kenny's face before my eyes. Just like Jett, he was sexy, tattooed, and had trouble written all over his forehead. The two of them were best friends. On the few occasions when I had met Kenny, he had been distant, taciturn even, so it came as no surprise that I barely knew anything about him.

"I'm sorry," I said when Sylvie remained silent, playing with the spoon.

"Don't be."

"He probably has a good excuse."

"More like a lame one." She checked her cell phone and shrugged. "You're so fortunate, Brooke. Your lucky stars have sent you a good guy. Knowing my crappy luck, my soulmate is probably some loser who's too busy playing video games to find me. In all seriousness, though, I'd rather have your problems than be stuck with a guy who doesn't have time for a relationship. Trust me, I'd rather be in a relationship with the prospect of getting married in five years than in one with a status saying indefinitely undefined."

Chapter 14

THERE WAS SOMETHING depressing in knowing Sylvie was unlucky in her love life when I was the one with the perfect boyfriend. Okay, Jett wasn't perfect. He had the perfect body, the perfect dimples. He knew how to give me mind-blowing orgasms, and he was sexy as hell, but he wasn't perfect...because he hadn't proposed yet.

If he'd just go down on one knee and ask, with a ring in his hand or not—I sure wouldn't mind as long as he just asked—he'd be more than perfect. He'd be a dream come true, because nothing sucked more than being untied and raising a child alone, all while being deep in a financial pothole.

"Things will change, Sylvie," I assured her in the most

serious and convincing tone I could muster. "If it doesn't work out with Kenny, someday, somewhere, someone will come knocking on your door and blow you away."

"Hopefully sooner rather than later, while I still look young and I can get them young. There's no way I want to be an old cougar," Sylvie said, trying her best to infuse some humor into the situation. "Don't worry about me. I'll be okay. As I've always been. I just need to go on a few more dates."

"I'm not saying you should give up on Kenny yet."

"I wasn't planning to." She smiled, tilting her head. "But I'm also not giving up my partying ways. If he isn't here most of the time, and can't be bothered to call, I'm not wasting my time waiting for Prince I-Can't-Care. I'm keeping my options open. So, for the time being, he might just have to share me with others." She touched my arm lightly, and her chirpy voice began to reflect her worry.

"Brooke, I totally get your fear with Jett. But it will be Thanksgiving soon, and your mom still doesn't know about him. She doesn't even know that you're pregnant, for that matter. Maybe you should stop thinking about marriage and instead start worrying about how to tell her. You can't avoid her for the rest of your life, you know."

Oh crap. Mom.

Double-crap.

Think of all the explanations and endless interrogations

I would have to endure.

Obviously, I hadn't forgotten to tell my mom about Jett and the pregnancy. I had just pretended to myself I could pull it off, that there would be plenty of time later. Simply put, I had been postponing the inevitable.

My temples began to throb. I hated being questioned, and in this instance my mother wasn't so different from Sylvie, maybe even a little worse. The questions would start at as soon as my mother realized I had found a new job and inherited an Italian estate, which had been the home of a kinky sex club. Then she would go on about me dating my boss, who just so happened to be the father of my unborn child.

Try to explain that to someone who insisted you had to drown in endless motherly love. Someone once said that a mother's love is unconditional. I wasn't so sure that applied to my mom, but the point was: too many incredible things had happened—incredible as in over the top or impossible to believe—and I had no idea where to start.

First, like any mother, she'd worry about my mental well-being, and suggest that I move back in with her. Second, she would ask so many questions that I'd end up having a headache for the rest of the year. And third, she'd judge the fact that Jett and I weren't married and yet we were having a baby.

"I won't say anything to her if you don't," Sylvie said

conspiratorially, "but surely you realize the moment the baby's born it might just be too late?" Now she was making fun of me. I grimaced but said nothing.

"Oh, for crying out loud." Sylvie rolled her eyes in mock annoyance. "Just keep it simple, and tell her over the phone so you can hang up and blame it on a bad connection."

"It's not that easy." I took another sip of my now lukewarm cappuccino and began to trace the edge of the cup with my fingertip. "It needs to be done in a public place, where she won't dare throw a hissy fit. You know her. If she doesn't like Jett, she'll be upfront about it, and I can't have her insulting him."

I knew she would; after my father's death, she lost all trust in the male population…and people in general.

"You mean like the one time she told me I've got no talent for karaoke?" Sylvie grinned.

"Yes, and I was mortified." I cringed inwardly.

My mother had an honesty about her that could pierce even the sturdiest of all armors. Granted, Sylvie was a little tone-deaf, but no one had the right to tell her that. With Jett, it'd probably be a little worse, her honesty more brutal, because there was a difference between sexiness and being pretty. With sexiness came power, which my mother equated to breaking a woman's heart. Jett had that particular look about him, that impressive confidence and sexy charisma that screamed sex god, and I doubted he could play those down.

"Besides, she lives in Philadelphia now, so I can't even pretend I don't have the time to drive over."

"Tina moved to Pennsylvania?" Sylvie asked, faking surprise.

In truth, it wasn't that much of a surprise. My mother moved around a lot, depending on the guy she was dating.

"When?"

"About a month ago." I let out an exasperated sigh. "You know her. New guy, new place."

Sylvie let out a laugh, and I couldn't help but join in. Years ago, my mother had been different, but after my father's death, she had sworn off any sort of commitment—an attitude I had adopted before I met Jett.

"Who's the lucky guy this time?" Sylvie asked.

I shrugged, signaling that I had no idea and no wish to find out either. She wouldn't be holding on to the new flavor of the month long enough to make it worth remembering his name. "I think he's Scottish."

"Another one?" Sylvie eyes bulged. "That's the fourth in a row. Seems like she favors them. You know, you could ask Jett to fib a little about his ancestry."

"Don't exaggerate. There have only been two." I bit my lip to stop my laughter, but failed. "And Jett couldn't pull off a Scottish accent if his life depended on it. He can barely hide that Southern drawl."

Sylvie's lips twitched. "Can you imagine him saying 'Yer little bloody scud, yer aff yer heid'?"

I almost choked on my laughter. Sylvie was great at imitating accents, and in particular British ones, which she had picked up on family vacations.

"You should be an actress," I said. "You're so good that I didn't even get half of what you just said."

"Yeah, I should, even though my family would probably disown me. You know how old-fashioned they are."

Sylvie's entire family was not just old-fashioned, but also wealthy. Old money. That was one of the few things I knew about them, because Sylvie never talked about her past.

"There's always YouTube," I said. "You could make a lot of money with parodies, and they'd probably never find out."

We chatted some more, until Sylvie checked the time and grimaced.

"Shoot," she said. "I wish I could stay, but work's calling. Got to look at some fucked-up reports."

"Oh."

I watched her get up and squeeze into her expensive coat before handing me a brown paper bag. "I've brought you your mail. Someone named Judy—or June or Julie or something like that..." She snapped her fingers in thought, then gave up. "Anyway, whatever her name, she's been calling a lot. She said she needs you to get back to her as soon as possible." Sylvie pointed at the bag again. "There's a letter from her in there."

"Thanks."

It was already after 3 p.m. when Sylvie leaned in to give me a friendly kiss on the cheek. "Call me if you need anything."

"I will." As I watched her leave, I felt a strange coldness creeping up my body again.

Chapter 15

AFTER SYLVIE WAS gone, I turned my attention to the stack of letters and hope surged through me. Whoever contacted me via email, might work at the legal firm, and might have sent me a letter to tell me more about the offer I had received for the Lucazzone estate. Leaning back, I began to sort through them.

Among the letters was a stunning fuchsia envelope, decorated with glitter, lace, and a satin ribbon, which I could only assume was another invitation to a college friend's wedding.

Lucky girl.

I banished the dark, envious thoughts that were still lurking in the back of my mind and pushed the envelope back in the bag, then went through the usual brochures and ads next—anything but the frighteningly white envelopes that looked way too familiar. Eventually, I finished sifting through the meaningless stuff. When I didn't find a letter that carried the Wighton & Harley logo, I had no choice but to turn my attention to the ones that mattered.

Even though I told myself there was nothing to worry about, my pulse started to race as I tore open the first letter and my eyes scanned the writing down to the bottom, where it was signed by a Judith Altenberg. I figured she was the woman who had called.

Miss Stewart,

After repeated attempts to contact you, I'm asking you to get in touch with me in regard to your missing payments over the past few months. Your overdraft has exceeded the limit, and we can no longer allow withdrawals. Your total debt has accumulated to a total of $49,867, and...

I stared at the number, stunned and paralyzed, unable to continue reading.

Fifty thousand dollars of debt.

And that was just the money I owed to the bank.

One bank.

Oh God!

How the heck did I—a twenty-three-year-old with a

baby on the way—owe that much to a bank? But even as I asked myself the question, I knew the answer. I wasn't born rich. Living and studying in New York City had been expensive. There had never been another option but to take out loans to fund my college education and to keep myself afloat. After finishing my education, I went through nine months of unemployment, during which I maxed out all my credit cards, then ended up working for *Sunrise Properties* with a salary that barely covered rent and food. When Jett hired me, he offered me twice what I had made before. But with a new job came the need for a new wardrobe and other expenses in order to fit into Jett's world.

I shook my head grimly.

Fifty thousand dollars was almost the price of a brand new car, something I desperately needed to replace my beloved *Volvo*, which had served me well, but it was now becoming a bit too unpredictable.

It was almost as much as Jett had paid with a single swipe of his card for a weekend at the TRIO hotel.

Dread threatened to choke me as I opened the second letter with shaking hands. Then the third and then another one. They were all reminders of my debts and student loans, accumulating to a whopping...

Ninety...

What!?

Ninety thousand dollars of debt.

My mind froze, and for a moment, I thought I might just throw up all over the floor.

What did you think, stupid? That your money problems would go away just because you have a well-paying job now? That not picking up the mail would make the bills vanish?

I felt physically sick, as if someone had just punched me twice in the stomach and left me lying on a cold floor, only to return with a truck, ready to run me over.

I had worked so hard all my life. Why couldn't life just give me a break?

In one angry motion, I balled the letters up, and pushed them across the table, as far away from me as possible. Even with my new promotion and the great bonus package, it'd take me forever to repay all of those loans while I struggled to keep my head above water. I buried my head in my hands and took deep breaths, but they didn't do much to calm me.

There were some possibilities, a few other options, like asking Jett for help. Or trying to find a way to change Alessandro Lucazzone's will and sell the property I had inherited in Italy. According to Jett's lawyers, the estate would begin to incur annual property costs and taxes, starting the following year. Only—even if I managed to find a clause that allowed me to sell the property—I didn't want to touch money that didn't really belong to me.

But the worst part was that Jett had no idea about my

money problems. No one knew, because I was too ashamed to admit it even to myself, let alone to those who cared about me.

The sinking hole wasn't getting smaller. If anything, I felt as though it was about to swallow me up whole. No matter what, I had to find a feasible solution.

Maybe start my own business?

I groaned inwardly at the thought. That would require another, bigger loan for starting capital, and my credit score was already scary as hell. Sell some personal items?

Maybe...but what?

I had nothing valuable, except for a few pairs of boots and some business attire that had seen more work than a lumberjack.

I snorted at my brain-dead ideas.

It wasn't just that most my clothes were old. I had been borrowing clothes from Sylvie for years and couldn't possibly sell the few new items I had bought with my last paycheck.

Asking my mother, who had debts of her own to pay off, was out of the question. Asking Sylvie, after she had been covering a larger portion of the rent for years (she always insisted) to help me out, was unacceptable. I realized that asking Jett for help was out of the question, too, even though ninety thousand dollars would have probably been like ninety bucks for him. He might be the rich boyfriend, who wouldn't even notice that kind of money missing from his account, but asking him would be like admitting that I was poor, and that I didn't fit into his world. Besides, I refused to be dependent on Jett; the only thing worse than being single or desperate was to owe a man. I couldn't live with the guilt and the shame, and especially not with the knowledge that, at some point, he might start to resent me or to look down on me. I didn't want money or lack thereof to define me.

The icy knot in my stomach intensified at the thought of having no means to fully provide for my child while I kept pretending to everyone that life couldn't be better. Sooner or later, with all the expensive trips Jett insisted on taking and his need for a lavish lifestyle, he was bound to notice that I couldn't keep up with him. And what would his rich and famous friends and clients think of me? Probably that I was a gold-digger, using him for his money.

I shuddered at the idea of anyone thinking that. It had been hard pretending to Jett that in my free time, I was going shopping when all the while I spent my time with things I could afford, like reading the free newspapers, talking free walks, and chatting for free with Sylvie via Skype. Basically, all things that were free. Sooner or later, he was bound to notice.

There was no question whether I wanted to grow up. I literally *had* to, and quick, if I was going to solve my problems. If I just knew how.

I drew a long breath and let it out slowly, but my heart continued to slam into my ribs. My stomach was still a frozen mess, and my brain frantically searched for a solution. Maybe I could discard all the letters and pretend I never received them for the sake of calming myself, because obviously stress wasn't good for the baby. Come to think of it, it wasn't such a bad idea. I could leave them on the table or trash them outside. Once they were gone, it would be like they never existed, and I could pretend for once that I didn't have the problems I had. That would give me both the clarity and the time needed to figure out my next move.

Or maybe, if I prayed hard enough, the banks might just make a mistake and transfer a huge sum of money from someone else's account into mine, which would help me gain more time to repay them, say in fifty years.

I sighed inwardly.

God, that would be so cool... but immensely unlikely. As in entirely impossible.

From the periphery of my eyes, I noticed the barista inching closer to my table. I looked up and found her gazing at me with a worried expression on her face. She wasn't much older than me. Her glossy black hair was held together by a girly red flower clip, and her nametag read "Thalia."

"Everything okay?" she asked.

I hated that question. More often than not, it required the need to lie, and I didn't want to. Not today. Not when I was hormonal.

Biting my lip, I smiled, even though I doubted I could fool anyone.

"The coffee's great. Thanks."

"I wasn't talking about the coffee," Thalia said, definitely not fooled.

Instant shame burned through me at the thought that she presumed I was on the verge of having a mental breakdown and might be about to cause her trouble in her place of work. I wondered how scary it must be to encounter an apparently mentally unstable customer who liked to crumple letters and throw them across the table. She clearly feared she might have to kick me out, or that I'd throw a hissy fit—or worse.

"I've seen better days." I smiled again and waved my hand dismissively, as though almost one hundred grand in debt wasn't a big deal. "But don't worry. I'll be gone in a minute." I stuffed the letters inside my bag and reached for my coat.

Only, too late.

"Look, I don't mean to pry, but I just thought…if you need work, we can always use an extra hand around here during the week from one to five." She pointed at the cashier. "She's the manager. I'm sure she'll give you the job if you tell her you're in trouble."

I stared at Thalia, open-mouthed. "How did you know?"

She pointed at my bag. "It wasn't hard to guess. I have experience with that kind of mail, and the red 'final notice' warnings on the paper made it pretty clear, even from across the room." She paused to watch my expression.

I just nodded, too shocked and embarrassed to say anything.

She took a deep breath and continued, "What I'm trying to say is I know how plain annoying banks can be. A job here might help."

For a few seconds, I remained stunned. My smile turned bitter as I realized that even a second job as a barista or waitress wouldn't solve my problems.

"I really appreciate the offer. It's just..." I moistened my lips, carefully considering my words so I wouldn't offend her kindness. "Well, I'm already working full-time with more unpaid hours than I can count. Even if I had the extra time to work a second job, it wouldn't pay enough to repay my student loans."

"I see." She scanned our surroundings quickly, as though to make sure no one was sitting close enough to hear us, and then she turned back to me with a facial expression I couldn't decipher. "You need more money? I know how you could repay your loan quickly, without having to quit your job."

I narrowed my eyes at the word "quickly." I didn't like quick. Quick was never good because, for some reason, I associated it with danger and illegal activities, such as robbing a bank. Unfortunately, my curiosity was piqued, if only to know what she was getting at.

"How?"

"You're a pretty girl, and I know someone who needs a pretty face." Her voice dropped to a conspiratorial whisper, which didn't help diminish my suspicion at all. "It's a good job. All you have to do is pose for photo shoots."

I frowned. "Shoots?" I asked in disbelief. "Are you talking about modeling?"

"Yeah." She smiled. After another quick glance behind her, she slid into the seat opposite from mine and leaned forward. "Sexy, provocative photo shoots. All you have to do is pose and look pretty. Consider it freelance work; basically a bonus that pays as much as three jobs would here," she said, pointing around her.

I almost choked on my coffee at the word "provocative."

Okay. Not a dangerous job—just...indecent.

It was almost as bad as I thought.

I couldn't possibly pose naked. For one thing, I didn't possess that kind of confidence, and for another, my body was currently going through major changes. I figured no one wanted to see those.

"I'm not really comfortable going nude," I said.

"Heard that one before." Thalia laughed out loud before her voice dropped to a whisper again. "I'll be honest with you. Obviously, nude shoots will make the most money in this profession, but that wasn't what I meant. I'm talking more along the lines of working as a pin-up girl."

"Oh." My mind conjured up pretty girls dressed in fifties garb, dangling on a swing, maybe even leaning against a vintage car.

Thalia nodded again, and a glimmer of enthusiasm flickered in her eyes. "It's really great. The photographer picks the costumes. You get to wear them, and all you have to do is pose and have fun. In a way, you become art. With your looks, you could easily pull it off."

Unconsciously, I smoothed the hem of my dress. It didn't sound bad at all, but her compliments made me a bit self-conscious. "Why would you think that?"

"You're sexy and young, without being obtrusive. You have curves in all the right places. My boss goes for that feminine shape, sometimes even big."

Big?

Had she just called me fat? I stared at her, both impressed and intimidated by her honesty.

"The official casting was last Monday, but maybe Grayson will consider giving you a test shoot if I talk to him and explain your situation. If he hires you, he'll pay between two and five hundred dollars an hour. And if you're really good and in high demand, you can make up to two grand per shoot, maybe even more."

My eyes popped wide open.

Holy shit.

I had always thought models weren't paid well. Two thousand dollars an hour was insane.

"That much?" It was more a statement than a question.

"I know! It's awesome, right?" Thalia's face lit up with enthusiasm.

I had no clue if her euphoria was because she loved her job that much or if the idea of helping me appealed to her. That just brought up the question as to why she wanted to help me and if the job was really as simple as she made it out to be. Regarding her for a moment, I took in her flawless, light brown skin, perfect makeup, young facial features with brown, almond-shaped eyes, and the way she had professionally styled her hair. She wasn't just a beautiful woman with a curvy body and dimples whenever she smiled; she was also someone who cared a great deal about her appearance. I wondered if I could be like her, not just to feel better about my pregnancy, but also to solve my financial problems in the process.

"If you don't mind me asking," I began, smoothing my hair back slowly, "why are you still working here if modeling pays so well?"

For a moment, she looked away, as though she was considering whether to tell me the truth. "Quitting here isn't an option. My youngest brother has leukemia. We need every extra dollar for his bone marrow transplant. Besides, there's also the health insurance I get here."

"I'm sorry about your brother. I had no idea," I said, feeling awful for prying into her personal business.

Thalia shrugged. "I don't mind working two jobs. I like it here. I get to meet interesting people, like you." She smiled gently. "Two years ago, I never thought I'd be a pin-up girl, but I was miles in debt and had a hard time finding a job that would allow me to take care of my family. Then I met Grayson, and he asked if he could photograph me. It was either that or..." She trailed off, leaving the rest to my imagination. "I had no choice but to take it. The offers come irregularly, but when they do, the pay is better than anything else I could be doing, because Grayson is well known in the industry, and his photos are always in high demand. Is modeling something you can envision yourself doing?"

I blinked at the sudden question addressed at me.

"To be honest, I'm not sure," I said, my thoughts running wild. "I've never considered it."

Not least because I most certainly didn't have model measurements. In fact, I was far from it. Besides, I didn't really know what pin-up girls did, and I had never posed for art.

"You don't really need to have a talent for it, but you do need to be natural. Like I said, you're basically paid to stand around looking sexy. Makeup and clothes will take care of the rest," Thalia said. "I'm heading over to meet with Grayson after my shift. Why don't you join me? I suggest you have a look around, see what I do, if you like it. Then you can make up your mind."

I had to admit: a modeling job that could pay so much without me having to take my clothes off was tempting. It wasn't a bad idea at all, especially if I just had to stand around while being paid for it. I figured whatever I made could go toward my loan repayments. In my position— what with me working long hours for Jett's company while being pregnant—I didn't have a lot of choices. Besides, the sooner I got out of debt, the faster I could reach my independence. Feel and be free.

But was I really model material?

Even as I asked myself the question, my heart lurched with fright. I hated being on display, and even more being the center of attention. The job was probably not even half as good as Thalia made it out to be. And even if this Grayson guy offered me the job, how would Jett react? Then again, what if it was the solution to all my problems?

My mind was spinning with options, and my heart thumped harder at the prospect of leaving all my financial troubles behind me, of breaking free from the chains of debt. Thalia's enthusiasm was definitely contagious, and as she said, I had time to decide. I could accompany her and see where it took me. But Jett could be back any minute, and if I wasn't there, he'd start asking questions. The modeling gig had to wait, at least for the time being.

"Do you mind if I give it some thought?" I asked. "Today's just not a good day."

"Sure. Take your time." Thalia retrieved a pen from her pocket, and wrote down some numbers on the note along with her name, then passed it to me.

"Call me whenever you're ready." She got up and reached out her hand. "I'm Thalia, by the way. What's your name?"

After everything that had happened in my life, I didn't like questions. They felt personal as if answers demanded to give up pieces of oneself; as if revealing the hidden parts of oneself, handing over the key to one's world, giving people permission to take what wasn't theirs. They were an invasion of personal space, and as such had to be avoided at all costs.

"Jenna," I lied, choosing my sister's name. The moment the word left my lips, I wished I could take it back. Only, it was too late to admit that I had chosen to pretend I was someone else.

She shook my hand. "Jenna, I know we don't know each

other, but I know this. If you decide to work with Grayson, you won't regret it. I can promise you that."

I wasn't so sure about that as I watched her depart with the same steady steps, ready to serve the next customer.

Jenna kept echoing in my head. From all the forenames I could have chosen, why the hell did I go with my dearly departed sister's name? As I gathered the remaining letters and stuffed them into my bag, I realized giving Jenna's name had seemed like a good idea in order to protect my own identity. But not so when her face still haunted my dreams. My sister was the one thing that had kept me going all these past years, when the journey had become rough. Her memory had also been the one thing that had kept me caged and frightened, wary and alone…until I met Jett. But it was that one simple wish—a thought, a need—to bring her killer to justice that would eventually release my soul from the pain of losing her, and set me free.

Then, finally, the healing could start.

Chapter 16

THALIA BARELY PAID me another glance when I grabbed my coat and handbag, and headed out into the cold to make my way back to the hotel. As the chilly air seeped under my coat and cooled my head, my wits slowly returned.

Seriously, what had I been thinking?

Modeling to solve my debt problems?

Really?

The longer I walked, the more the idea seemed ludicrous, conjuring all kinds of images in my head, like creepy men and money scams. By the time I reached the hotel, I was convinced that Thalia received a commission for finding gullible girls and reeling them in. People didn't just help others unless they had a heart of gold—and let's face it, the world wasn't exactly full of those. Most people had ulterior motives or selfish agendas, and Thalia was probably one of them. I had read about one of the dirty sides of the modeling business; the one that operated under the pretense of offering great jobs, right after one paid for having an expensive portfolio created. Once the money was paid, the jobs would never roll in. Thalia had been as convincing as a trained salesperson, but I wasn't about to fall for any tricks. When something sounded too good to be true, it probably was.

I entered the gigantic lobby and stopped, considering whether to head upstairs to the penthouse and try to open the locked suitcase or head for the shops and buy something to wear and surprise Jett at the office...when I remembered that my credit cards were maxed out.

Dammit.

"Welcome to reality, Stewart," I mumbled.

Not only were my debts messing with my life; they were also ruining my chance to buy something sexy and new, if only to feel better.

I never thought I'd miss my old room resembling a matchbox, but a few weeks into living with Jett and seeing his walk-in closet, which was larger than an entire store department, and I felt like asking Sylvie to let me move back into our tiny abode, just so I could pick and choose from her stuffed-to-the-brim wardrobe. Sylvie had so much stuff—thanks to her family's platinum VISA card—that she hardly remembered what was in her closet. Such a surplus would have come in handy at the moment, if only to get out of the dress I was wearing.

I had almost reached the elevator when I noticed a redhead dressed in black heading in my direction. I recognized her as the receptionist who had greeted me upon my arrival the day before.

"Miss Stewart?" she said.

I nodded.

She handed me a large envelope. "This letter was left for you an hour ago."

"Thanks." I watched her walk off, her dress shoes click-clacking across the marble floor, before I turned my attention to the envelope. There was no address; not even a room number. Only a name, printed in capital letters:

BROOKE STEWART.

My heart pounded in my chest. Apart from Jett and Sylvie, no one knew where to find me. I figured it had to be from Jett, even though he could have just called me instead.

Was he trying to surprise me with yet another game?

He could be quite creative when it came to our sex life. But, even for his standards, this felt a little surprising, and for some reason all I could think of was that maybe...just maybe...this was one of those days that would end in a proposal after all.

Granted, Jett thought marriage should feature in one's cards only after at least half a decade of dating, but weren't miracles known for hitting you when you didn't see them coming? A girl could dream.

I sighed. If Jett only proposed, I wouldn't even need a proposal like the ones you see in the movies. I'd take a hand-written note, a hint, or anything at all.

With shaky hands and a half-smile on my lips, half expecting the cameras to roll on me, I tore the seal open, my heart threatening to jump out of my chest. As I pulled out the sheet of paper, I frowned and eventually my smile died on my lips. A cold shudder ran down my spine.

Oh, my God.

That couldn't be.

Chapter 17

AS I SCANNED the letter in my hand, another cold shudder ran down my spine and then the shock came slowly in thick, long waves.

This couldn't be right. It just...couldn't be.

In my hand was a piece of paper titled, "Visitation Log," and on it was a long list of dates. Disbelief washed over me as I stared at all the times Jett's name popped up at one and the same address.

Six weeks.

Twice weekly.

In prison.

Jett had been visiting his brother in prison.

My heart thudded against my chest as my throat

constricted. I didn't know what to think, what to make of *this*—of what it was supposed to mean. My pulse raced at the thought of Jett meeting with *him*, of all people. Sure, he was my boyfriend and my boss, but wasn't he supposed to tell me this little fact—after everything that had happened?

I turned the paper in a feeble attempt to find out who had sent the list, and for a second, my heart stopped, and my legs threatened to buckle beneath me as nausea gathered in the pit of my stomach. I stared at the words as if they belonged to another language, but there was no mistake. Right there, it clearly stated—in black and white:

Freed, on the grounds of a lack of evidence.

It had been signed two days prior and stated that Jonathan Mayfield, who was known to everyone as Nate, was to be released within twenty-four hours. That placed his release the previous day—which was right when Jett and I had arrived at the TRIO hotel.

Gripping the wall for support, I closed my eyes and inhaled a deep breath, but the air felt stuffy, as if it contained no oxygen. I felt so weak that I feared I might just pass out on the spot, and the walls would come crashing down on me.

"It's not possible," I muttered to myself.

That just *wasn't* possible. It couldn't be because in the past few weeks I had not once considered the possibility. Of all the things I had feared, his immediate release had featured nowhere in my mind, nor in my imagination, not even in my nightmares. My hands were shaking so hard I had to ball them into fists. The magnitude of the words hung heavy in the air.

The sword of Damocles dangling from a thin thread above my head.

Fear and anger threatened to choke the life out of me as I read those words over and over again in the hopes they might somehow dissipate into a figment of my imagination if I begged them long enough.

Jett's brother, Nate, was free—the very man who had kidnapped me, hurt me with the intention to kill me, and then had sent Jett's father into a coma. In my mind, I could see the images happening in slow motion: Nate holding a knife to my throat, the blade slowly penetrating the thin barrier that was my skin. He was a monster, a cold-blooded killer with a sick need to inflict pain.

How the fuck could Jett visit him?

He might not care about how I felt about Nate, but what about the things Nate had done to his own father? And, most importantly, why did they release Nate?

My fingers gripped the paper so hard it crumbled in my hand.

It wasn't so much the pain of the past, of what had happened, of knowing that Jett could still face this man, but the shock at the realization of what might now lie ahead, of what I had been hoping would never repeat itself. I had been trying to forget and run from the past for so long that it had taken every ounce of my willpower not to let things get to me. And now a serial killer was a free man.

My God!

Nate might be after me this very minute, eager to get his revenge for all the trouble I had caused. The evidence I had found was supposed to tie him down for a lifetime. That they let him go didn't make sense. Unless Nate had connections, someone who helped him find a loophole.

A killer who had run an illicit club.

And now he could continue with his previous crime spree—raping innocents, killing for sport like a hunter would chase after a fox.

My throat constricted at the thought, and the trembling in my limbs intensified. As the black pit from my past slowly opened beneath my feet, threatening to engulf me once again, I realized my past efforts to control my fear had been in vain. Suddenly, the shiny marble floors of the TRIO hotel didn't look relaxing at all. They looked like they were about to crack like stones.

Was it possible that Jett didn't know about his brother's release?

Possibly, but not likely.

He'd visited him so often. Surely someone would have told him during one of his regular visits. He had to have known it. Anything else wouldn't make any sense.

With the envelope clutched to my chest, I rushed to the front desk. The receptionist was summarizing the hotel's amenities to two guests.

"Who sent this?" I asked, cutting in front of them, hardly able to contain my voice. Even to my ears, I sounded hysterical. Knowing this, I tried again, this time calmer. "You gave me this envelope." My voice still trembled with shock as I showed her the envelope. "Someone left it for me. Who was it?"

She stared at me for a moment, confused, and then her eyes widened as recognition crossed her face. My heart pounded so hard I feared it might be about to burst.

"It was left for you this morning, ma'am." She turned to a man to her right. "I wasn't here, but my colleague was."

From the way he was standing, rigidly observing the entire situation, I concluded that her colleague was actually her superior.

He stroked his beard and shook his head slowly. "I'm sorry. I didn't see anyone. It was given to one of the bellboys, who delivered it to the desk. I'm afraid the sender left no name," he said in a deep voice.

The female receptionist nodded and turned back to me, repeating the man's words. "I'm sorry." She then turned her attention back to the couple, apologizing for the disruption.

I stared at her. Under different circumstances, I would

have complained that they weren't more forthcoming. But seeing that I was the one disrupting their service to the guests, and they were just trying to do their jobs, I mumbled weakly to the waiting couple, "I'm sorry," and then walked away.

Once I reached the elevators, I stopped, unable to ignore the rising panic inside me. Leaning against the cold tile wall, I stared at the envelope, unsure of what to do. Someone had wanted to deliver a message. Their mission had been accomplished.

Did it really matter where or who it came from?

Whoever sent it had wanted to tip me off, all the while choosing to stay anonymous. I figured the person was someone who knew Jett well; someone who was familiarized with Jett's working schedule, and probably knew Nate, too, which wasn't so surprising. Before his incarceration, Nate had been on the board of Mayfield Realties. That the sender knew where to find me bothered me, but the more I thought about it, the more I realized that I needed to talk with Jett. Until then, none of it was going to make sense.

I speed-dialed his number and waited. The line rang until it went to voicemail.

Pressing my hands back into fists, I couldn't stop another wave of anger from gushing through me. Couldn't he sense my distress? Jett usually picked up on the second ring, unless he was in a meeting or conference, which, I assumed, had to be the case.

I stashed my phone back in my handbag, only to pull it out a minute later. I didn't know what made me punch in one of the assistant's number. I reckoned it was out of desperation and the knowledge that doing something— anything—was better than doing nothing. As the phone kept ringing and I waited for her to pick up, I prayed that the message in my hand was nothing but a joke, some kind of stupid, thoughtless prank, and Jett would set it straight.

Emma picked up on the second ring.

"It's Brooke," I said by means of introduction. "I need to speak with Jett, please."

There was a short pause before Emma answered in her usual snobby tone. "He's off work until Wednesday, as you know."

I blinked several times in succession. Of course I knew that tiny detail...only he had cut short our weekend to return to work, and that was a detail she should have known.

"He's not there?" I asked, incredulously.

"No, Brooke, he's not." Emma's voice was thick with sarcasm. "Aren't you supposed to be on a vacation *together*?"

Was that a hint of glee I detected?

I clamped my mouth shut to keep back a venomous remark. The woman was full of contempt, and it wasn't just a personal issue she had with me. She had once dated Robert Mayfield, Jett's father, and for some reason, she had the impression that it somehow entitled her to be bitchy. The tension between us had always been thick as smoke. For a long moment, I pondered if she could have been the one who sent me the envelope, if the glee I detected in her voice actually stemmed from her delight at me being in the dark while she held all the cards.

Since I wasn't sure, I decided to proceed carefully.

"We are. It's just..." I paused, grasping for words. "Jett wants to know if everything's fine."

She paused, her hesitation palpable.

"I see." Not even pretending to hide her disappointment, she heaved an exaggerated sigh. "Let me check."

Papers shuffled audibly in the background, and then the line fell completely silent. For a moment, I wondered if she had put me on hold, keeping me waiting on purpose. The seconds stretched on forever, until I was sure Emma would never return.

Finally, something rustled in the background. Candy? Last time I had checked, the candy bowl had been in the lobby sixty stories down, which meant my gut feeling had been right. She *was* keeping me waiting on purpose.

"Nothing to report," she said, after what felt like an eternity. "Tell Jett everything's fine. We're managing perfectly well without him."

I winced as the noise of foil wrappers carried down the line, then a chewing sound echoed in my ear, so loud I had to keep the phone away. It wasn't hard to imagine Emma chewing with her mouth open. She knew it got to me, and that was my fault. A few weeks earlier, in an attempt to break the ice by having a little chat, I told her that I'd once shared an office with a guy who always distracted me with his noisy eating.

When I could bear to put the phone back to my ear again, I rolled my eyes and put on the sweetest voice I could muster. "Great. Thank you, and have a good day, Emma."

I disconnected before she could answer. As much as Emma's hellish and childish behavior annoyed me to no end, my thoughts were on something much more grim: Jett wasn't at work, and I was worried that something bad had happened to him, which might have been the reason why he wasn't answering his phone.

By the time I returned to the reception desk, my heart was pumping hard, this time with yet more worry. The redhead gazed at me with a patient expression, as though she had been expecting me. She was probably used to dealing with annoying guests like me.

"Hi," I said and smiled sweetly. "Do you happen to know when Mr. Mayfield will be back? We're staying in the penthouse suite."

I almost expected her to shake her head and offer a curt, "*No, sorry,*" just to brush me off, but instead, she pulled up her eyebrows in recollection.

"Mr. Mayfield is booked in Conference Room 5A for this afternoon." She pointed to the open entrance to her right. "Follow the hall, then turn left. You should find him there."

I stared at her, open-mouthed, as the images of horror in my head slowly dissipated and turned into something else: red, boiling fury.

He hadn't been in an accident. No need to start making calls to all the hospitals in New York City. I couldn't have been happier about that, but I also couldn't have been angrier at the newest development in his actual whereabouts.

"He's...?" My voice failed me, and for a second I was about to lose it.

He had been here all along.

The reality hit me hard and fast, knocking my breath out of my lungs.

"Conference Room 5A," the receptionist repeated. "Would you like me to show you the way?"

She eyed me with sympathy, as if she could sense my distress. Or maybe she was just used to female guests being disappointed by rich men. Either way, she suspected that

I'd had a hard day. What she didn't know, though, was that my day had not just been hard; it had been a living nightmare, and I was worried it was only going to get worse.

I shook my head in response. "Thanks, but that won't be necessary."

I headed in the direction she had pointed, barely paying attention to the expensive paintings or the polished marble floors. My feet walked fast, as if something was chasing me, as if my life depended on it. In a twisted way, something *was* chasing me: the past I had hoped would never catch up with me.

If this is a dream, God, please... please let me wake up.

The prayer was futile, though, because it wasn't a dream. No dream I had ever had felt so surreal, yet was real, and I knew I wouldn't be waking up from this living nightmare, no matter how many times I tried to pinch myself.

I had a bad feeling about Nate, not least because he was a killer on the loose. Countless questions kept spinning in my mind, all of which I hoped Jett could answer. The sooner I met with him, the faster I could secure the water dam, before the flood burst through and swallowed me whole.

I crossed the hall and took a left, toward the conference rooms. The area was quiet, almost serene, decorated with huge arrangements of orchids and a plush, red carpet that hushed the sound of my heels.

Conference Room 5A was the last door to my right. Even before I stopped in front of it, I noticed that the doors were wide open, and it was awfully quiet.

A rush of disappointment surged through me. No one was inside, meaning the meeting was over. I entered nonetheless, and sat down at the ridiculously huge, round, mahogany table that would have made King Arthur's knights proud—in ancient business times.

The faint smell of coffee hit my nostrils, making it clear that the room had been recently occupied. But by whom and why? Who did Jett meet here, and why would he hide it from me?

Chapter 18

MY HEAD WAS a blurry, spinning mess. So many questions, so few answers, but among them the one question that kept burning inside my mind: why would Jett lie to me about being at the office when he was right here, in the hotel? And, most importantly: why hadn't he told me that he had been visiting with his brother—the very man who had tried to kill me—in the past few weeks?

They were little lies, but lies nonetheless. For some reason, I kept thinking that maybe Jett didn't know his brother had been released.

It was possible.

Hard to imagine, but still possible.

I had to believe that...for the sake of our relationship

and our baby.

However, in the event he had known about it, what prevented him from telling me? My fingers traced the smooth surface of the mahogany table as my mind fought hard to put the pieces together.

The letter...Nate's release...Jett's secrecy.

Nothing made much sense.

Unless, of course...

Another cold shudder ran down my spine. I tried to stop the dark thought before it could invade my mind, but it was too late. My breath came ragged and heavy. The assumption made me sick to the core, and I grasped the edge of the table for support.

Nate wanted the Italian estate I had inherited, just as Jett had wanted it when he hired me. While the two brothers had different, if not opposite, motives, with Nate greedily wanting it for himself, Jett had just sought to preserve the company reputation and ward off the scandal. Of course that was all before he got to know me better, and fell in love with me, after which he proclaimed he had no interest in it anymore. I once chose to believe him and gave him another chance, trusting that he was on my side.

But what if I had gotten it all wrong from the beginning. What if...Oh God!

My fingernails clenched the table, scratching into the finish of the wood as my mind conjured up another option with bigger implications—something that would be awful beyond my wildest dreams.

I shook my head. The thought was horrible and yet it sounded too plausible to be immediately discarded.

What if Jett was *still* after the estate?

Maybe...when the first plan didn't work out, he decided to play a new card, a cleverly concealed ruse: gain my trust while pretending that his brother and father were the ones not to be trusted, all the while supporting them, being on their side, fighting for the bad guys, seeing that he and his family had the same goal. After all, some say blood runs thicker than water.

If that was true, I wasn't safe anywhere and with no one. I bent forward, rubbing my hands over my knotted stomach.

No, it couldn't be true. The mere thought was crazy, utterly insane.

I had it all wrong.

I smiled bitterly as waves of nausea rolled through me. If I didn't put things in check, get them into perspective, I would morph into a compulsive madwoman, unable to decide whom to trust and whom not. Taking deep breaths, I recalled all good reasons why my fears were unfounded:

First, Jett had saved my life on more than one occasion. Were it not for him, I would have been dead. If he wanted me gone, he could have used one of those opportunities to get rid of me.

Second, years after leaving the gang, Jett had sought out his former friends to help me.

Third, there was also the fact that he loved me. He had told me so on numerous occasions. I knew words didn't always mean much, but when he had said it, I had felt it deep within my heart. Maybe my feelings had betrayed me, but for some reason, I just knew he had spoken the truth. And then there was also that small, unrelated matter: Nate had shot his father. I'd seen it with my own eyes. Surely if it was all a plan, there would be no need to endanger a family member's life.

Unless the person was a psycho.

And Nate was a psycho all the way.

For a long time, I just sat there, the seconds stretching into minutes while I fought to clear the mist inside my head. Eventually, I came to the conclusion that there had to be a different reason why Jett had not been upfront with me about Nate. I could feel it. I was so close I could almost grasp it—if only I could think clearly and figure out the one piece of information I knew was missing in order to solve the puzzle.

Under normal circumstances, I could have dealt with anything and anyone. But today I needed a drink, if only to calm down my nerves and get rid of my excruciating headache. I decided it was safe enough. Just one glass of wine, and then I'd return to the suite and wait for Jett to have *the talk*.

Chapter 19

CLUTCHING THE ENVELOPE to my chest, I headed for the hotel club, thankful for the fact that it was in walking distance. By the time I arrived, the club was dimly lit and half-full of patrons. I headed straight toward the bar and sat down on a bar stool near a group that looked to be part of a bachelorette party. Clad in my slutty dress and high heels, I blended in perfectly.

I waited impatiently for the bartender, my finger tapping in the same rhythm as my racing pulse. It was in that moment that I heard a familiar voice saying, "Brooke can't know about it."

I froze instantly, my eyes scanning left and right, though I struggled not to crane my neck or spin around. At first, I thought it was just my imagination, a figment of my creative and anxious mind, but then my eyes fell on *him*.

My heart skipped several beats.

Standing close to the bar, almost obscured by a huge abstract ice sculpture, was Jett. Even in the semidarkness, with the beautiful glass chandeliers hanging so low they almost touched the tables, he stood out with his broad shoulders and dark hair I'd recognize anywhere, anytime.

Holy mother of pearls.

What was he doing here? The reasonable thing would have been to get out before he saw me. Only, I wasn't exactly the reasonable kind.

The bartender approached me to take my order. I pressed my index finger against my lips, shushing him, then cautiously craned my neck to get a better view.

Jett was sitting at a table near the bar. Opposite him was a woman, her back turned to me, so I couldn't see her face. But from the way she leaned forward, gesticulating animatedly, I knew they were having an interesting conversation.

She seemed to be the only person he was talking to.

My heart lurched in my chest.

The picture before me was like poison, killing me softly as it coursed through my body. Self-preservation kicked in, urging me to get away. And yet I found myself inching closer to the monstrous ice statue, thankful for the privacy it provided. It was the only way to catch more than fragments of their conversation; the only way to find out who she was and why Jett was leaning too close to her, hanging on to her every word.

"You sure this is what you want, Jett?" Her voice was young, maybe twenty-five. It was also deep and sultry. Intimate, I realized. They were calling each other by their first names, clearly knowing each other. I dared to crane my neck just a little bit more, but all I could see was long, black, glossy hair and toned arms.

"I'm sure." His voice carried the same determination and stubbornness I had grown to accept from him. "I've been waiting for this for a while now, and to be honest, I don't know a better time."

The woman nodded, as though she knew what he was talking about and couldn't have agreed more. "Because she doesn't know?"

"Yes," Jett said slowly.

My pulse raced harder.

Know what? Waiting for what? They were talking about me and thought I didn't know *it*. I frowned. After everything I had discovered throughout the course of the day, I didn't like this one bit, especially the part involving me not knowing. I regarded the woman intently in a desperate attempt to figure out who she was. Dressed in an elegant, golden cocktail dress, she didn't look like one of

Jett's uptight business associates. They were talking quite openly about me, so I figured she had to be some sort of acquaintance.

So, a friend. Or maybe...

I swallowed hard, not allowing the disturbing thought to enter my mind.

Had he met her by accident, bumped into her on the way back from his business meeting, and she so happened to know about our relationship?

Maybe she was a friend from college or a client he had met on the job, and now they were discussing the best way to market her property. The explanations sounded plausible enough.

Silence ensued between them, and for a moment, I wondered if I should show myself; pretend as though I had just entered and spotted them. But then, all of a sudden, she shifted in her seat and ran a hand through her long, black hair, spreading it around her like a beautiful velvet curtain.

"Do you remember last year?" Her voice dropped so low I could barely discern the words. "You and me?"

She and him?

What the fuck was that supposed to mean?

My blood began to boil as a pang of jealousy hit me with full force.

This was no mere acquaintance. It didn't exactly take a genius to figure that one out.

"Don't tell me you never miss it, Jett," she continued.

My pulse raced faster as I watched Jett's reaction. Regarding her with an unreadable expression, he was his usual composed self. Seconds passed by. I bit my lip hard, wishing he'd say something—anything that would give away his true thoughts.

A shrill yelp, followed by female laughter, echoed from my right, startling me. The bachelorette party was slowly coming into full swing. I wished they would just shut up, but my unspoken plea came too late. The woman turned her head in reaction to the drunken squeals, and for a split second, I thought my heart would burst.

I knew that woman.

Oh my God.

I knew her.

Chapter 20

"OH SHIT," I murmured under my breath. My hand pressed against my mouth as shock registered in my brain.

It was Tiffany, the girlfriend of one of Jett's friends.

What the hell was Jett doing with her here?

After Nate's attack on me, Jett and I moved to live with Jett's former friends in an effort to ascertain there was always someone around to keep an eye on me, and keep me safe. Brian, being Jett's oldest friend, had made sure everyone accepted me; his girlfriend, Tiffany, however, was the one who seemed to have a problem coming to terms with it. She had been extremely hostile not only to me, but to Jett as well, which was why I had always tried to avoid her. Her hostility had seemed strange to me, but I had assumed it was because of Jett's past fallout with Brian. Now I knew my explanation had been implausible, if not a ridiculous assumption. Seeing them together made so much more sense. She had been jealous back then, because she was dating Jett and probably thought she had a claim on him.

A strange sense of foreboding crept over me at the way the two were sitting—too close for normal friends, too close for anything—talking about their past. A past I knew nothing of and probably shouldn't have been eavesdropping on. A past I would have been better off not knowing, if only to stop the images beginning to flood my mind.

I watched the way she looked at him, the way I always looked at Jett—full of admiration and something else.

Lust. Longing. Desire.

Love.

Had I been so blind that I failed to see Tiffany wanted Jett, too?

The realization kicked me hard and fast that whatever they once had, it wasn't over. She definitely wasn't over him. And maybe he wasn't over her either.

Vaguely, I remembered the text message Jett had received that morning. It had been signed with "TI."

TI standing for Tiffany. A tiny pang, like a shock to my heart, shot through me as I realized that it had been Jett who asked her to meet with him. Not the other way around, which made all the difference. Why would he do so if he was dating me?

Unless...

"I know you better than anyone out there, Jett," she said after a long pause. "Look at me and tell me in all honesty. Can you really say to my face that you don't miss it? All the things we did? All the fun we had?"

My throat tightened when her fingers began to trail up his arm confidently, as though they had done so countless times before, as if her hands belonged on his body. It was a gesture intended to coax an answer from him. Manipulative but intimate nonetheless. I'd be a fool not to think that after what I had heard and seen already.

Like being strapped in a tower chair high up in the air, my body was rooted to the spot, unable to move. I was forced to look on, watching the scene unfolding, unable to do anything except for waiting in fear.

Waiting for what?

For his answer? For his reaction? To see my heart breaking of knowing too much? I had always been interested in discovering more about his past, but now I wasn't so sure if my curiosity hadn't been more a curse than a blessing.

"It's over, Ti. You know that," he said with less determination than you'd expect from such strong words.

Even to my ears, his tone sounded weak.

Judging from Tiffany's half-smile, she didn't believe him either. She leaned forward again, and let out a short laugh.

"You said the exact same thing last time, but you forget that I know you, Jett. The real you." She inched closer to him, her voice sexy and low as her fingers traced up his arm again. "You aren't the kind of man who is happy with just one woman in his life. You admitted that when you left me after two years. You said success and winning mean everything to you, that you always want more."

I held my breath, my nails cutting through the frail barrier of my skin. It bothered me that Jett didn't brush her off, that he simply remained quiet instead of setting her straight. It bothered me that he'd let her touch him like that, as if he enjoyed it. But what bothered me the most was the fact that he had met with one of his exes behind my back.

Actually, bothered was an understatement.

Inside, I was burning with uncontrollable, gut-wrenching rage, hating the fact that Tiffany had three things I desperately wanted: a history with Jett, knowledge about his past, and obviously enough trust that he could talk with her so openly about me.

She must have felt she was being watched, because she turned, and her eyes scanned the room. For a fraction of a second, I thought our eyes connected. Her eyes narrowed in surprise, and ever so slowly, a faint smile spread across her lips, as though she was happy to discover she had an audience. It was then that I knew for sure she had seen me.

What a bitch.

She knew I was dating Jett. She knew we were expecting a baby, and yet she still met with him behind my back.

I wished I could scream, shout, or walk over there and confront Jett—do anything rather than just stare at them— but strangely, I felt devoid of life, as if the knowledge that even if I interrupted their little meeting, it wouldn't have stopped Jett from wanting to see her in the future, nor would it have meant that whatever they had was over.

Maybe I was meant to see them. Maybe, just maybe, it was all some misunderstanding that could be easily cleared up.

My ears kept ringing loudly as I watched Jett reach for his glass to take a sip, his actions slow and hesitant, reminiscent of the past. I knew I should leave before it was too late, but for some reason, my legs wouldn't obey my brain's command. With each second and word, with each glance they cast at one another, the pain in my heart intensified. My brain, now dripping with forbidden knowledge, swirled the bitter thoughts around, pumping more poison through my veins.

"I miss the times when we were young," Tiffany said quietly. "We were in love, and we had that amazing chemistry. I know we haven't talked about this in a long time, but…" She paused as she regarded him. Her fingers brushed her eyes gingerly, as though to wipe away unshed tears "But sometimes I wonder what would have happened if I had kept the baby; if things might have taken a different turn."

Oh, my God.

A baby? His baby?

She had been pregnant by Jett.

The realization hit me like a train: whatever they had in their past must have been special—like what I had thought I had with Jett. Or maybe even more special, considering that she had been dating him for longer, and that was probably the reason why she hated me. She likely felt I'd taken him away from her, that I was the other woman, an intruder in their relationship.

A rebound.

Staring at her, I tried to swallow the thick knot in my throat. It tasted as bitter as her words and equally piercing.

Jett had never told me about the baby or his relationship with Tiffany, nor had he revealed that he was seeing her behind my back. He had betrayed my trust once before, and now he was doing it again. I buried my fingernails in the soft skin of my forearm, eager to inflict physical pain in the hopes that it might drown out the shock of his betrayal, and block the images of them together—a nightmarish vision I never saw coming.

Judging from Jett's hard features, he seemed completely taken aback by her words. I never knew what jealousy meant until I experienced the heart-shattering, soul-wrenching pain of seeing Jett with another woman and not being able to do anything about it. And not only was she another woman, she was also his ex, someone he'd almost had a baby with.

"Our room is ready for us. It's the same we used last time," she whispered and rested her hand at the nape of his neck. And then she smiled...not at me, but at him...as if he was the only person in the room. It was a special kind of smile: soft, tender, almost fearful.

"There's always a new beginning, Jett," she whispered. "You wanted to see me, and that's all that matters. Deep down, I knew we were never over. That you'd come back to me someday."

As I watched her lean into him again, my throat constricted from the urge to scream, but no sound came out. The ice-cold feeling in the pit of my stomach turned into a raging storm as her hands pulled him nearer: so close, too close.

Finally, their lips locked in a kiss.

I was so shocked I couldn't breathe. A jolt of pain pierced my heart—thick and sharp as a blade, right in the middle of my chest, as though I had just been stabbed, and the knife was being pulled out slowly, ripping through

tissue, creating a wound so big that nothing could ever stop the bleeding.

I pressed my hands over my mouth, unable to stop the tears from running down my face like little rivulets, and eventually, my disbelief turned into bitter grief.

I had to get away—*now*, as quickly as possible, before my fragile soul shattered. My legs began to move of their own accord as I ran out the door, past the drinkers and diners who looked up in surprise. I ran right out of the hotel, trying to get far away from the one person I'd fallen in love with, the one person who had destroyed every inch of my faith in love and relationships.

My head spun with the images of Jett kissing another woman, a woman who hated me because she wanted him.

I had to get away, because I couldn't bear to see him anymore, without feeling the stabbing pain whenever I thought of his lips on hers, gentle, just the way he kissed me so often; without wishing to get shot that instant, if only to stop the pain, my love for him, and the images I knew would haunt me for the rest of my life.

Jett had been the best thing that had happened to me, but after today's discoveries, he had broken me more than anything or anyone ever could. He had shattered my heart beyond repair by seeing her behind my back. He had betrayed me with her, and for that I hated him. I hated him for that even more than for visiting a killer behind my back.

Hated him like I had never done before.

How dare he kiss her when he was still with me?

After everything that happened, after everything we'd gone through, his actions hurt even more than when he had tried to trick me to get the Lucazzone estate. The realization hit me that nothing would ever be the same again between us. There was no doubt I would never be able to look at him again without the images of betrayal flashing before my eyes. I would never be able to face him again, to look at him and not see her.

The dark thoughts I had tried to suppress crept back, ridiculing me. They were more welcoming now in the comfortable mist of my dark mood. This time I shuddered, not from the cold, but from the possible connections I hadn't grasped before: like the possible fact that Jett had sided with his brother, withholding the evidence that so clearly would have kept the psycho locked away forever. Or the fact that Jett had always been too good to be true. If he had kept a few secrets from me, what's to say there weren't many more? Why not include the ploy to earn my trust in order to benefit his hidden agenda?

Love had made me blind. All he had to do was tell me a few lies, pretend to be in love with me, and make an utter fool of me in the process.

When a lie was involved, there were usually two sides to the story. My mind could have adjusted to the idea that a fact was either true or false. However, in Jett's case, where he had clearly pretended our love was true, and that he cared about me—which had turned out to be a lie—then went behind my back, spinning a story about his brother, and about how much he loved me, there were still multiple facets I didn't know about him. Jett was a preteniar, a pretender and a liar all rolled into one, and I liked the idea of calling him what he was.

Angrily, I wiped the tears from my face, but more followed in mascara rivers. He didn't deserve a single tear. He didn't deserve my love or my self-pity. The bastard deserved nothing.

As perfect as he had seemed at first glance—sweet in words, gentle in actions, and sexy as hell—I shouldn't and wouldn't forget the fact that I had always sensed something dark lurking inside him. It was a side I had always been afraid to confront or face.

It wasn't only my inability to trust that had prevented me from giving him the promise he so desperately sought. More than that, deep down, I had always sensed that he was never really serious about me, and I couldn't make promises of any kind to a man like him; a man who had always been too good to be true.

Now I had to get away from him. There was not a single doubt about that. This time, I swore to myself that I would stay away from him—no matter what. It would hurt like hell, but I knew I possessed the strength to move on with my life. I had to…and if I couldn't do it for myself, then at least I would do it for my child.

END OF EPISODE 1

Jett and Brooke's story continues in the powerfully sensual next part in the No Exceptions series,

THE

LOVER'S

GAME

COMING SEPTEMBER 9TH 2014!

THE LOVER'S GAME (NO EXCEPTIONS BOOK 2) SNEAK PEEK

CHAPTER 1

The street was abuzz with life, the noise of traffic and human crowds droning in my ears. Tears trickled down my face in steady rivulets, as though my body was connected to an ocean. My legs carried me so fast, at some point my feet began to hurt and I realized I had been running. And yet I didn't stop, not even when my lungs began to burn from the cold air and the lack of oxygen. It was only when I reached a bench in Central Park, the one where my sister and I used to sit ten years ago, did I stop and slump down, grateful for the cold, snow-covered wood that numbed my body.

He had broken me into pieces. The stupid fool I had been for falling in love with him, how could I have taken him back after he had betrayed me only to betray me again?

And to think that he had told me I could trust him; that he loved me; that I was the only one in the whole world for him, and that he would never cheat on me.

Yeah, right!

They were stupid lies I had believed and wanted to come true. Someone should have offered me a personality test and marked me "naïve, foolish, and let's not forget, prone to being broke." When she had named me Brooke, my mother apparently forgot to remove the o on my birth certificate, because now I wasn't just broke of money; I was also devoid of some much-needed wisdom—if only to see Jett for who he was when I had viewed him through rose-colored glasses: a cheater and lying bastard who was still seeing his ex behind my back. Sylvie had been right when she had warned me to be careful around him. I just wished she had shaken some sense into me rather than gush about his good looks all the while counterpointing by pointing out that he was bad news, which was counterproductive. It hadn't exactly helped me ward off his past advances, except to make me want him even more. His intensity had pushed me into a state of obsession, where desire became addiction and hunger my passion. If it weren't for my longing to be loved, I would never have been so blind to his intentions.

I didn't know what hurt me more: the fact that I had trusted him blindly—as in only seeing what I had wanted to see in him, trusting that he'd never lie or cheat on me. Or that he had actually done all the things he had promised he wouldn't do behind my back. And I hadn't even seen it coming because I had chosen to believe his promises.

Sexy men like him don't deserve another chance, another glance, another surrender. They deserve to have their ass kicked, and not only out of bed.

I couldn't wrap my mind around the fact that just a few hours ago, I had been happy. Truly happy. There had been no warning—nothing— to indicate that my life would be turned upside down. Even if I had wanted to, I couldn't have seen the events coming. There had been no signs to prepare me for what had happened, or for all the feelings that had just crushed me to the core.

Minutes felt like they had turned into hours. I didn't know how long I just sat on the bench, oblivious to the people passing by and the curious glances they cast my way. But at some point the cold began to creep up my body, intensifying the shudders running through me. I had never been so cold in my life and yet I had never welcomed the numbing pain more than now. The cold numbed not only my limbs; it seemed to penetrate every layer of my being. But I had reached a point, where I didn't care what happened to me, if I froze to death or if the world came to an end.

Everything had started out so well and now I was in so many ways back to square one: single, heartbroken, and broke—except I was a little worse off than before. In the beginning, I could have walked away from Jett in the hope that my heart would heal. I would have moved on to the next man eager to get into my panties, and wouldn't have needed to hide from shame.

But now I was pregnant and while I had inherited the Lucazzone estate with all its money and dark secrets, those facts also added to the problems I couldn't run away from. With Nate freed, I still had to fear for my life.

The dark thoughts…

Come to think of it, there was no sense in believing in an *us* anymore.

The only thing that mattered now was keeping myself and my child safe, and the only way I could accomplish that was by getting far away from Jett and his family. But to accomplish that, I needed money. Even with my faith in men and ever finding true love ripped to shreds, I could feel that my discovery was a blessing in disguise. The pain was going to be temporary, but the entire experience would serve a greater purpose because I finally knew which path to take.

I opened my handbag in search for the piece of paper that was my beacon of hope. I had to give Thalia's job a try, because any job, as long as it paid the bills, was better than none. If only a tenth of Thalia's claims were true, then I had found a way to get away from here, from him, from everyone—a fresh start. Once everything calmed down, I'd focus on healing my heart and move on from a past that wasn't worth remembering.

End of sample

Never miss a release. Use the chance to request Jett's POV or get a sneak peek, teasers, or win amazing prizes, such as an e-reader of your choice, gift cards, and ARCs by signing up to my newsletter.

As a subscriber, you'll also receive an email reminder on release day:

http://www.jcreedauthor.blogspot.com/p/mailing-list.html

To those, who want to learn more about Brooke's past and the story behind the Lucazzone estate, I welcome you to read the prequel of No Exceptions:

SURRENDER YOUR LOVE
J.C.REED

A THANK YOU LETTER

There are so many things I want to say at the end of a book, but in the end it all comes down to two words:

THANK YOU.

As some of you know, NO EXCEPTIONS was never supposed to be written, but after the conclusion of the Surrender Your Love trilogy many readers contacted me to ask for more, and I decided not to let go of Brooke and Jett yet. In The Lover's Secret, I have spun a new story of love and loss, a new mystery, with the intention to create a new a standalone series.

As you continue to read the characters' story, you will learn that love *always* survives, but sometimes it takes you in a completely different direction than you initially thought.

To all of you, who have read or plan on reading, my books and to all of you who have spread the word: I can't thank you enough for your support and love for my stories. I want to thank each and every reader out there for giving this book a chance. I want to thank the wonderful bloggers I now have the privilege of calling my friends. I want to thank my fans, who took the time to write reviews. I want to thank my amazing editors and cover artist for all their hard work and for putting up with all my last minute changes. Lastly, I want to thank my little munchkins for understanding that mommy's busy writing a book in the wee hours of the night. And, finally, I want to thank God for allowing me to meet amazing people like you.

Thank you. Thank you.

I love you all.

Jessica C. Reed

Connect with me online:

http://www.jcreedauthor.blogspot.com

http://www.facebook.com/pages/JC-Reed/295864860535849

http://www.twitter.com/jcreedauthor

22297762R00126

Printed in Great Britain
by Amazon